JENNY'S TEXAS COWBOY

JENNY'S TEXAS COWBOY

•

Linda L. Paisley

AVALON BOOKS
NEW YORK

PRINTED IN THE UNITED STATES OF AMERICA
ON ACID-FREE PAPER
BY HADDON CRAFTSMEN, BLOOMSBURG, PENNSYLVANIA

To my children, Julia, Joseph and James, and their spouses.
For your encouragement, which came in a variety of forms,
I am lovingly grateful.

Chapter One

Joshua Brady pulled into the parking spot designated for the CEO of Starr Enterprises, and turned off the purring motor of his red Corvette. He unfolded his tall, lithe frame from the cradle of the driver's seat. Grabbing his briefcase and laptop computer with one strong, tanned hand, he firmly set his Stetson hat on his head with the other. Sun-lightened strands of thick brown hair nearly touched the white collar of his shirt. As he dropped the car keys into the pocket of his trousers, he reached for his brown, Western-cut jacket and slung it over his shoulder.

With a few long strides, he reached the private elevator that would whisk him to the executive floor of the Starr Building. This floor was the

1

nerve center of the real estate and construction business Joshua had inherited only three short years earlier, when both parents died in a private plane crash. Now one of the youngest CEO's in the country, he was proving his worth in Dallas's corporate world. People close to him knew that his heart still remained on the family ranch, the Brady Belle, that lay a hundred miles north of Dallas in the Red River country of north Texas.

The Brady family had ranched there for several generations. Josh's father, Adam, ran it successfully for years, while enlarging its land holdings and improving its herd quality. When Adam married Amelia Starr, the only daughter of a prominent Dallas real estate tycoon, few thought the marriage would last. But the city girl and country boy complimented each another. They combined their businesses and enjoyed nearly thirty happy years together, before their untimely deaths.

Josh had just returned from a long weekend at the ranch, which accounted for the tuneless little whistle escaping his pursed lips. Though he knew old Gabe had a steady hand on things at the ranch, every so often he felt the need to spend some time on the piece of ground he loved. This had been one of those weekends, and his soul felt refreshed. The home-cooking of Gabe's wife, Consuela, was a need he liked to assuage often as well.

Stepping out of the elevator onto the Spanish-tiled floor of the spacious reception area, he mentally prepared himself to get back to the high-pressure business of running the corporation.

"Good morning, Mr. Brady," murmured the newest receptionist. The neat-looking, attractive blonde wore a turquoise suit, smiled shyly and turned back to her switchboard, which had indicated two calls coming in simultaneously.

"Mornin'," Joshua answered with a nod, as he continued walking to his office. *Good*, he thought, *she seems better able to keep her mind on the job than her two predecessors.* He'd be glad when Sylvia, the regular receptionist on the executive floor came back from her maternity leave.

The others hadn't been fired but discreetly moved into the secretarial pool away from Joshua's office by his sympathetic executive secretary, Emily Jordan. Joshua's presence seemed to turn their normally good work habits to mush. More than one of the single women working at Starr had been impressed by his rugged, handsome, cowboy looks, not to mention the attraction of the wealth and prestige he enjoyed.

Joshua wasn't immune to the smiling glances or the bolder overtures of some of the young ladies in his employ. But he had determined to keep his private life separate from his business when he had taken over the reins of Starr several years earlier than he ever thought he would.

Still single at thirty-one, he most decidedly wanted to do his own looking. After a disasterous relationship in college, he was cautious of city girls. He hoped to meet a woman who preferred ranch life. His father had been lucky with his choice of a city girl for a wife, but Josh considered his parents a definite exception to the rule.

Tossing his Stetson onto a wall rack, he hung up his jacket before striding across the lush beige carpet to his mahogany desk. Sitting in the comfortable brown leather chair, he swiveled toward the large corner windows behind him. The Starr Building sat across the street from a municipal park that separated the cluster of office buildings from an historic district of restored Victorian homes. He spent a few moments enjoying the view before he reached to press the intercom to his secretary's office next door. Before he could speak into it, Emily had opened the connecting door and briskly approached his desk.

"Welcome back, Josh," she said in a friendly voice, as she placed the morning mail into a neat pile at his left elbow. When Joshua inherited his father's office and title, Emily Jordan came with it. Joshua would be forever grateful for her help in smoothing the transition when he had to take over so suddenly.

"Mornin', Em." He flashed a broad smile her

way, something he rarely did around the other women in the office.

Emily returned his smile as she sat in a chocolate brown chair across the desk from him. Crossing her trim legs, she tugged her grey suit skirt into place, before settling back in the plush chair. An attractive older woman with silver hair worn in a smooth chignon, her grandmotherly appearance belied her astute business sense, though in fact, she and her husband were proud grandparents of four.

"I hope you enjoyed your weekend out at the ranch, Josh. Things have been pretty quiet here, though there are several letters that will need your attention," she stated in her no-nonsense way.

"Uh-huh," he agreed. "What's the status on the possible deal with Broadwater?"

"All the up-to-date info is in that file," she answered, indicating a fat file on the left corner of his desk. "If there's nothing right now, I'll get back to work."

Joshua spent some time looking over the information Emily had left before dictating into a small tape machine. He then dove into the thick Broadwater file, making notes as he went, only coming up for air a few hours later.

Buzzing the intercom to Emily's office, she came in as requested. Joshua handed her the file.

"Please type up these notes, Em. I expect I'll

be meeting with Broadwater soon." He also handed her the tape from his dictations.

"Shall I set up a meeting for later in the week?" she asked. "And would you prefer a lunch meeting or to meet here in the office?"

"I think the Danford to start," he replied, referring to a prominent restaurant. As he stretched his arms over his head, flexing his shoulders, he caused a muscle to ripple under the fabric of his shirt.

Emily turned to go back to her office. Repressing a giggle, she thought she didn't blame the single girls for chasing after their handsome boss.

Checking his wristwatch, Joshua picked up the newspaper folded neatly within reach and swung his snakeskin boots onto the edge of the desk. Shaking open the paper, he scanned the front page and studied the business pages for a time, before turning to the sports section.

Checking some scores, he was about to turn the page when a note in a column jumped out at him.

"Damn," he muttered aloud as he returned his boots to the floor, and he sat forward reading intently.

Former champion bullrider, Chris Courter, and his wife, Sue, were killed recently when their pickup truck slid off an icy road near their ranch in Montana. Chris had made a name for himself on the college circuit a decade ago, then went on to win at Nationals in 1993 after he turned professional. He and his wife are survived by a young son and Chris's sister.

"Jenny," Joshua breathed harshly.

His mind flashed back to a picture in Chris's wallet of a cute little fourteen-year-old girl with thick, dark braids and laughing blue eyes under the wide brim of a white cowgirl hat.

She's alone, he thought, *and probably needing help.*

Joshua yelled for Emily.

"Goodness, what's wrong?" she asked, wide-eyed with concern as she stepped into the office.

"I'm going away for a while, Em. An old friend from my rodeo days has died in an accident," he jabbed a finger at the newspaper item; "and I want to check on his little sister. She's just a kid, and from what I remember, Chris and she had no other family but each other."

Emily picked up the paper and read what Josh had indicated, then turned back to him, awaiting instructions.

"Put the Broadwater deal on hold for now—string him along. I know that's easy for you. Right now, call Tony and tell him to fuel up the plane for Bozeman, Montana. I'll pack a bag and meet him at the airport in ninety minutes. I'm probably too late for the funeral, but I want to pay my respects and see how the girl is doing."

"Understood," Emily concurred. "Oh, I've typed the letters. Let me get your signature on them before you leave."

Scrawling his name on the papers Em brought from her office, Joshua checked the contents of his briefcase, picked up his laptop, jammed his hat on his head, and grabbed his suit jacket.

"I'll check in with you regularly, Em. I'll be back by the end of the week, but I'll let you know if that changes," he added with a frown furrowing his brow. "Tell Jack what I'm doing; he's in charge temporarily. But keep me informed of how things go."

Joshua gave Emily a high-beam grin with a twinkle in his eye as he walked toward the door. She smiled back.

"So long, Josh," she said. Already walking toward her office and her phone to put in the requested call, Emily wished him a safe flight.

"Thanks, Em," he said over his shoulder as he opened the door and strode through.

Tony, the pilot and airplane mechanic had been employed for a decade by Starr Enterprises. He had the corporate jet fueled, and a flight plan filed when Josh arrived by cab, having left his beloved Corvette in the garage at home.

Despite his parents' death in a plane crash, his love of flying had not been tarnished, and he enjoyed this time in the air. Though he made an attempt to do some work, he was distracted by memories and soon gave up.

He had met Chris Courter while in college. He was at the University of North Texas and Chris went to Montana State. Both rode for their college rodeo teams, and though fierce competitors in the arena, they had become fast friends. Josh was taking a degree in Business Administration and Construction Engineering to prepare him for joining the family business, while Chris was studying Agri-Business as he was already running the family ranch part-time.

Later, they met several times as both pursued the professional rodeo circuit. Their best year came when Chris won the Nationals in bullriding, and Josh took third in the calf-roping competition.

That night, over a few celebratory beers, Chris told him that he was leaving the circuit. His father was no longer able to run their ranch alone. But Chris whipped out his wallet to show Josh a photo of the girl he planned to marry.

"I met her at school. She's wonderful, Josh. She was raised on a ranch in Wyoming, so she knows how difficult ranch life can be, but she also loves it as much as I do."

Shaking his friend's hand, then pounding him on the back, Josh said, "You're a lucky son of a gun, Chris! I wish you a ton of happiness as a married man, but how did *you* lasso such a beautiful girl?" Josh studied the curly-haired blonde with a happy smile, and added, "She's probably much too good for you, old man."

Both laughed, and Chris said Josh was probably right.

As the wallet lay open on the table, Josh noticed the photo opposite Chris's intended and asked who the cute little girl was.

"Oh, that's my kid sister. Yeah, she's cute— mouthy, too! Loves to ride, loves the ranch. She's fourteen, now. Came along late in life to my parents . . . then Mom died when Jenny was nine."

He closed his wallet and placed it back in his hip pocket.

"That's tough," Josh commented.

"Yeah, it was, and now Dad doesn't have much longer, either. She'll just have me then. But she likes Sue, so we'll be her family."

Josh remembered that photo and the unusual tug he had felt when he looked into those laughing blue eyes. Then, he had dismissed the thought, as she was only a teenager—and a young one at that. But now, he suddenly realized with a frown, she must be twenty or twenty-one. Could even be married.

I've been thinking of her as a kid, he chided himself, *and she's far from it. She'll think I'm nosing into her private business, if I turn up now. Oh, well, I'll go slow. Check out the lay of the land and see if there's a need for help*, he told himself. A devilish grin lit up his rugged features, as he suddenly felt curious to see how the skinny teenager with the gorgeous blue eyes had turned out. Rising, he walked forward to ask Jay, Tony's co-pilot, about how much longer to Bozeman?

Tony Hidalgo and Jay Banks had landed safely in on that Monday in April. Tony parked the corporate jet where directed and went inside to file a return flight plan for the following morning.

Josh had phoned ahead from the plane for a rental car to meet them at the airport. He stashed his luggage and the pilots' overnight flightbags in the back of the Jeep Cherokee, and they soon found rooms at a local Holiday Inn.

Josh picked up a roadmap at the motel, and the three men went in search of a good steak dinner. They found it at a restaurant the desk clerk had recommended on Main Street.

The men enjoyed a long-standing friendship beyond their professional relationship. Talk of flying, the ranch, rodeoing, and Tony's two teenaged children flowed freely.

As they were savoring a last cup of coffee, Josh extracted the roadmap and unfolded it to show where they were. He traced the route that would take him from Bozeman to Turk, which was in Madison County to the southwest.

Tony asked as he sat back in his chair, "Any idea how long you'll be staying, Josh?"

"Probably just a few days. I figure I've already missed the funeral," he replied with a grimace, "but I want to take some time to look around, see how things are for Chris's little sister. She may be okay, but I know their parents are both dead. If Jenny's left with the ranch, and I assume she has been, she may need some help."

Tony guffawed. "Take it easy on the advice, amigo. There are few women—or men—who like advice pushed on them."

Josh laughingly agreed, "Yep, you're right. I intend to take it slow. I've never met Jenny, just heard about her from Chris years ago. 'Mouthy' is the word he used to describe her. Anyway, I'll be checking in with Emily," Josh added as he re-folded the map, "and I'll tell her when I'm heading back. The usual twenty-four hour notice okay?"

"No problem," Tony replied.

Chapter Two

Jenny pushed her long black hair away from her face. *Why didn't I take the time to braid it this morning?* she thought irritably. She knew the answer to that. She had been in a rush to feed and dress Chip, her young nephew, who had tried to feed and dress himself. Jenny encouraged his doing that, usually, but today she wanted to get away from the ranch and into town before Bart Jones made his daily visit to check on her and the boy.

It was true that her life had been upended by the accident that had killed her brother and sister-in-law. She was grief-stricken, but she had vowed to care for their little son no matter what it took. But she felt no need to have Bart Jones in her life as a result.

13

Perhaps Bart meant well, but yesterday she thought he'd never leave. Even her best hints didn't seem to work. So today, she wanted to hurry into town.

Once there, she and Chip took a stroll down Madison Street, the main street in the small town of Turk. She was wearing worn jeans, equally worn black boots, and a sheepskin jacket. A black Western hat sat firmly on her head. Chip walked along holding her gloved hand with his mittened one, the hood of his bright red-and-blue parka pulled up against the wind.

There was little traffic moving that morning, though several cars and pickups were parked near a restaurant, the post office, and a tractor supply store. Jenny heard children's laughter from the playground of the school a few blocks west of Madison Street. The school complex drew its students not only from Turk but from farms and ranches and a few smaller towns nearby. Jenny had graduated from the high school just three years earlier.

Jenny dropped Chip off at Beth Grayson's "Pooh Bear Daycare" for an hour of playtime before she did her shopping. Chip seemed to get taller every time she turned around, and she knew she should buy some new undershirts that would fit over his pudgy little tummy. *Going to be tall like his daddy,* she thought with a pang in her heart.

After leaving "Jackson's Western Wear," she crossed the street to the post office to pick up several days of accumulated ranch mail. The little bell on the door jangled as Jenny closed it behind her.

Tillie Ginn, the postmistress, came to the front desk from her rooms at the back of the old house. A tall woman past middle age, her salt-and-pepper hair was worn in a short, curly perm. She wore jeans with a red plaid flannel shirt hanging loosely over a black pullover. No one would call her handsome, but Jenny knew her to be one of the kindest women in town.

Tillie greeted Jenny with a welcoming smile that creased her face and lit up her hazel eyes.

Jenny returned the greeting, and got the mail from her mailbox. Quickly sorting through the handful of catalogs, bills, and sympathy cards, she extracted a larger envelope with a return address of the county courthouse and the name of a lawyer, Ned Newhouse.

Her hands shook as she ripped it open. Worrying her full lower lip with her even white teeth, she scanned it quickly.

"Everything okay, hon?" Tillie asked gently.

"Yes, I guess so. The wills are to be read at ten o'clock on Tuesday, the thirtieth. It seems so strange, Tillie. Both Chris and Sue gone so young. I'm even surprised that Chris *made* a will, he was never one to be bothered with formalities, but I guess after little Chip was born, he and Sue thought to do it."

"Well, don't be too concerned. I'm sure it's all cut and dried. Does Chip have anyone else who might want to raise him?" asked Tillie curiously.

"Sue had an aunt and uncle down near Sheridan, Wyoming, who raised her, but they're both gone now. I'm all that Chip has left, I'm afraid," she replied, her voice quavering briefly. Then she added more firmly, "But don't get me wrong, I love that little fellow, and I'll be happy to raise him."

Jenny wiped a tear that had escaped down her right cheek while she spoke, then gave Tillie a brief smile.

"Sorry, the tears just seem to come these days. Never used to cry," she said gruffly as she gathered her mail and turned toward the door. "I've got to stop at the grocery before I pick up Chip at Beth's place. I'll be seeing you,"

"So long, Jen," replied the postmistress.

Tillie heaved a sigh. *A world of trouble has been dumped on that girl's shoulders*, she thought. *Lord, we could sure use a miracle here. Jenny's a strong girl, but a little help would be fittin', if You don't mind me askin'.*

She turned back to sorting the bag of mail that had come into town on the morning truck run from Butte.

Nearly an hour later, Jenny had bought the groceries and loaded them into the trunk of her old blue car. She affectionately called the car "Baby," and it had safely taken Jenny back and forth from Turk to college classes at the university in Bozeman for three years now. She didn't make the trip every day. During the worst of the winter months, she shared an apartment with three friends during the week, but Jenny rarely missed a weekend at the ranch.

Next, she stopped by Beth's daycare. As Chip was stacking soft, large, colorful blocks with another boy his age, Jenny stood to one side and chatted with Beth.

"Chip's been very good today, Jenny. Not nearly so fussy as last week when he was here," Beth said matter of factly.

The thirty-something redhead shoved up the sleeves of her turtleneck sweater and sat down in a rocker while she kept one eye on her charges.

"He's doing pretty good. He still asks for Mommy and Daddy though, especially at bedtime. I feel so bad that I can't explain it all to him," Jenny admitted to her friend.

"It's such a shame, and so hard for a little child. But it's only been a few weeks. Chip will adjust."

Feeling the sharp prick of tears behind her eyes again, Jenny nodded in agreement, not trusting her voice just then. Yes, Chip would feel better in time, but how would she feel? Blinking her blue eyes rapidly to check the threat of tears, she mentally stiffened her backbone and smiled brightly when Chip looked up from the blocks and spotted her.

He scrambled up from the floor and scurried across the carpet as fast as his almost two-year-old legs could carry him.

"Jen-jen," he squealed as he grabbed her around the legs.

Jenny stooped to lift him into her arms and gave him a big hug.

"Hi, Chipper! Have you been having fun?" she asked.

"Yep, fun," he agreed with a grin.

"Good." She set him on his feet. "Now, let's find your coat and head for home. I have food to put away in the freezer."

Then, "Thanks, Beth, for watching him. I'll bring him back to play again in a few days, probably Thursday."

"Fine, I'll see you then," Beth replied, as she turned to little Cody who was unhappy that Chip was leaving.

Sue, Chip's late mother, had arranged for him to come to play twice a week at "Pooh Bear Daycare" for the past several months. Now, under the circumstances, Beth and Jenny felt keeping to the routine would be the best thing for Chip.

Josh was on the road that morning driving toward Turk. The weather was windy, and gray clouds were scattered across the sky, but here and there early spring sunshine filtered through and brightened the landscape.

This was Josh's third trip to Montana. He had participated in the College National Finals Rodeo on the Montana State University campus his junior and senior years. That had been nine or ten years ago. He remembered how he'd loved the rugged mountains then, and he was equally impressed now.

There was still a lot of snow on the mountains and piled along the road, though the highway was clear. For several miles it ran alongside a river— the Madison—Josh recalled from reading the map. Though fast-moving, ice still clung to areas of the riverbank—evidence of the strong grip winter had had on the land just a short month ago.

It didn't take much imagination to picture the road completely covered with snow and ice. He wondered if Chris's pickup had slid off the road somewhere near here.

With a shake of his head, he dismissed the thought. No use thinking of the accident. Over and done. More important now were young Jenny and the little boy.

As he pulled into Turk, Joshua looked around with interest. Not much different from a lot of small cowtowns in Texas. Trying to decide where to stop to ask about the location of the Courter Ranch, he spotted the Turk post office.

If anyone would know, he thought with a smile, *it'd be the local postmaster.* His mind flashed to the postmistress of Banjo, the dusty cowtown nearest to the Brady Belle Ranch in his area of Texas. Maybelle Jeffers always knew who was doing what to whom and where, almost before the people concerned. Joshua chuckled aloud as he pulled over and parked in front of the building housing the Turk post office.

As Josh stepped inside the bell jangled on the door. When an older woman opened the green curtains hung in a doorway to a backroom, he revised his description from postmaster to postmistress.

She paused a moment and eyed him curiously. Then, seeming to make up her mind, she walked through and took her place behind the old-fashioned barred window.

Josh touched the brim of his black Stetson in a salute. The postmistress gave him an answering smile.

"Howdy, ma'am," Josh said in a respectful manner.

"What can I do for you, stranger?"

"Well, do y'all know of the Courter place? I'd like directions to find it."

Noting the Texas twang in his voice, Tillie grinned and observed, "That sounds like Texas in your talk, cowboy. You're a long way from home. Why do you want to find the Courter Ranch?" she added with a little squint of her eyes as she gave him a measured look.

Seeing that look, Josh knew he'd have to explain before she'd cooperate, so he replied, "Yes, ma'am, I'm from Dallas, but I was raised on a ranch in the Red River country. The name's Josh Brady, and I used to rodeo with Chris Courter back in college and on the pro circuit for a few years. Just by chance I read of his passing in the paper, and I came to pay my respects."

Tillie looked more at ease. After all, she wouldn't have sent just *any* stranger out to Jenny's place, but this cowboy knew Chris, so she supposed it would be all right.

"Well, I'm afraid you've missed the services, Josh Brady, but I'll be glad to head you in the right direction. By the way, I'm Tillie Ginn and, as you can see, I'm the postmistress here." Her smile broadened as she stuck her right hand through the opening in the counter window, and Josh shook it.

"Glad to meet you," Josh said. "I'm sorry to miss the services. I figured I'd be too late. The piece I read in the Dallas paper implied that it had happened a few weeks ago."

"Yes, more than a month ago now," advised Tillie, warming to this young man. "It was a real shock to Jenny, Chris's younger sister, but she's holding up real well. She's a strong girl. She has to be, especially with the boy to look after now. She's got spunk, that one." She paused and studied him again. "You ever met Jenny?"

"No, I've never had the pleasure, ma'am, though Chris spoke of her a few times." Josh rocked his weight from one foot to the other as a sudden image of the photo of Jenny sprung into his mind.

"Actually, she was in this morning to pick up the ranch mail. She's likely back home by now. Now, you go south out of town and after about three miles, you'll see a ranch road—Turk Creek Road—going off to your left. Take it for about five miles and you'll find the Courter Ranch on your right. Can't miss it." Josh thanked the lady and bid her a polite farewell.

Tillie stood there with a bemused look on her face. When she had first come through the curtains, she had been stopped short by the rugged good looks of the tall stranger standing there. A Texan. She'd always been partial to Texans, and an old friend of Chris Courter's to boot, anxious to pay his respects to Jenny and little Chip.

"Well, Lord," she said quietly with a glance heavenward, "I asked you for a miracle for Jenny . . . I'm wondering if I haven't just met him. Thank you mightily, Lord."

Joshua drove south out of Turk, as Tillie Ginn had directed. The road was fairly straight for awhile. He could see a rugged mountain range off to his right and another to his left. Josh soon spotted the turn-off and steered the Jeep onto a dirt and gravel road.

The road wound over hills and came out into a valley that seemed to be at a higher elevation than Turk had been. *This is beautiful country,* he thought, as he looked at the mountain range that was now much closer. The land had been fenced on either side of the road with four-strand barbed wire. The first gate he saw led to the left and was marked by a sign reading "High Meadows Ranch."

A mile or so farther on, he found an arch over a road to his right. *This must be it,* he thought, as he glanced up and read, "Courter Ranch." Slowing, he turned under the arch and rattled over a cattle guard.

The sound, though familiar to a cowboy, jarred Josh a bit and he wondered why he suddenly felt nervous. He decided that courtesy bereavement calls made most people nervous, and concentrated on the scenery. There were rolling pastures on either side of the lane, and a stand of pine trees sheltering a big old house of weathered clapboard. A large barn and corral were to the left with several smaller buildings. While most looked in good repair, all were in need of a fresh coat of paint.

Pulling off to the right in the large front yard of the house, he clicked off the motor. He got out and walked up to the wide wrap-around porch. He thought it would be a hot summer day, but a gust of wind caused him to settle his Stetson tighter and turn up the collar of his jacket.

Josh paused on the first step leading up to the porch when he heard the bark of a dog and voices coming from the house. Not quite able to make out the words, he was only aware that they were male and female voices, raised in anger. Josh decided in a split second to walk around to the back of the house.

I know I'm sticking my nose in where it may not belong, but if that's Jenny, she doesn't sound too happy.

Chapter Three

With that thought, he rounded the corner and found himself in the backyard only a few feet from a glassed-in back porch. He stopped short and sucked in his breath. That had to be Jenny. He gazed raptly at a young woman in boots, jeans, a sheepskin coat and a black Western hat. She stood on the top step leading onto the porch, holding a little child tight in her arms. The wind whipped her long black hair into her face, and she impatiently pushed it back with one hand as she shifted the boy onto her hip.

The heated words she'd just spoken to the man died on her lips when she caught sight of Joshua. Her lips still slightly parted, a flush rose into her cheeks when their eyes met. Or was it just from the wind? He'd wondered how the skinny teen-ager had turned out, and now he knew. Spunky, like Tillie Ginn had said, and mouthy, as Chris had described her. Dang! She was pretty: slender, not very tall, with long hair, black as a raven's wing; a cute little turned-up nose; and inviting feminine lips. Josh's eyes and senses took in everything. He felt the same tug inside him, look-ing into those blue eyes now, as he'd felt when he'd seen her picture all those years ago.

They looked at each another for what seemed like forever but was likely only a moment.

When he realized he was staring, Josh shifted his eyes to the man standing at the bottom of the steps. A middle-aged man, he stood about five feet ten. He was dressed in the workclothes of a rancher, and he scowled back at Josh.

"What do *you* want?" he asked angrily, obvi-ously upset by the interruption.

"I've come to see Ms. Courter, and from what I've heard, she wants you to leave, pronto," Josh replied in a calm, smooth drawl.

"It's no business of yours, cowboy," the man replied with a sneer. "Just butt out!"

"No, Bart, I want *you* to go," Jenny put in firmly.

The dog, a border collie, gave another warning bark from where he crouched a few feet away. He looked gentle enough to Josh, but seemed ready to leap if anyone laid a hand on Jenny or the child.

Giving both Josh and the dog a baleful look, the man objected again.

"I'm not leaving you here alone with a stranger, Jen. No matter what you say."

"You know Zach is just down at the barn, now just *go*, Bart!" Her voice quivered with a renewal of the anger she'd felt just minutes before.

As Josh continued to stare at him, Bart turned and stalked to his battered green pickup, muttering under his breath. As he slammed the door, Josh noted the words, High Meadows Ranch, painted on the driver's door. Bart gunned the motor, and the truck flew down the lane.

The color in her face heightened even more as Jenny said, "I'm sorry about that. Bart's a neighbor who's been a little bothersome lately."

Goodness, where did this handsome cowboy come from? she thought, as she gave him a quick once-over from beneath lowered thick black lashes. Tall, strong and rugged was her quick impression of him.

Then Jenny remembered her manners. Shifting Chip onto her left hip, she extended her right hand to the man.

The dog, seeing Jenny welcome the stranger, came over and sniffed Josh's boots. Josh put out his left hand so the dog could get a good whiff of his scent; and, satisfied, the dog ambled off toward the barn.

"That's Matthew, watchdog extraordinaire, and I'm Jenny Courter. Thanks for the help. What brings you to the ranch?"

Josh took her slender but strong hand in a firm grip. He felt that tug in his heart again.

"My name's Josh Brady, Ms. Courter. I'm from Dallas," he replied, touching the brim of his Stetson with the fingers of his right hand. "I was a friend of your brother's. We rodeod in college and in the pro circuit together for a few years. I just heard of your loss, and I wanted to visit and pay my respects."

Jenny stared at him for a moment, before regaining some semblance of poise.

"All the way from Dallas, Texas?" she asked incredulously, intrigued by his husky drawl. "Well, come on in, Mr. Brady. Chip should be inside, out of this wind. It's stronger out here than it was in town, and I've got groceries to put away."

She turned and opened the door to the back porch and realized she was babbling. Something about this Texan jangled her nerves. Why was that? She slid Chip down to the floor, and he toddled off toward the kitchen.

Josh offered, "Let me carry in the groceries

while you stay with the boy." He held out a hand for the car keys.

She dropped them into his hand, deliberately not touching him again, and said, "Thank you, Mr. Brady. They're in the trunk."

"Be right back, and please, call me Josh." He flashed a broad grin at the young woman, who smiled in return.

"Okay, Josh, and I'm Jenny to my friends and just about everyone else," she replied a bit breathlessly.

While Josh was outside, she quickly shed her jacket and hat and hung them on the rack. Catching up with Chip in the kitchen, she helped him take off his parka before he dove into his toybox. Jenny hung the boy's jacket up near hers, and ran to the bathroom off the kitchen to run a brush through her wind-tangled hair. She stared back at the reddened cheeks of the girl in the mirror, and wished she had time to change her shirt.

You ninny, she berated herself, *don't go overboard. Just because he's about the cutest cowpoke you've seen in a long time, he's not interested in you. He's only here because of a long ago friendship with Chris.* But her heart differed from her head. Boy, what a great smile!

Back in the large kitchen, Jenny poked the fire in the old-fashioned iron range and added a piece of wood cut from a dead apple tree. She turned on a large blue-enameled coffeepot. She liked to keep a pot going in case Zach wanted to come in for a cup sometime during the day.

As she did that, she heard Josh at the door and hurried to help him open it.

Within a few minutes, Jenny had put her groceries away, and Josh had hung his jacket and Stetson on the rack next to Jenny's and Chip's. He took the chair she offered him at the large, round table in the center of the kitchen. Josh looked around and observed that the iron cookstove must be used mostly for warmth. It did make the room toasty.

Pale sunlight shone through the blue curtains and onto the blonde curls of the boy as he played by his toybox. Nearby was a padded wooden rocker set below a mantel of polished oak that held an antique clock, a pot of ivy, and several ceramics.

When the coffee was ready, Jenny set a mug before Josh and moved the sugar and creamer bowls closer to him.

"Thanks, Jenny. This coffee smells great," he added as he stirred two spoonfuls of sugar into the mug.

She smiled over her shoulder, then reached to pull a pretty glass plate down from a higher shelf in the cupboard.

Moving across the room to an antique kitchen cabinet from her great-grandmother, she filled the plate with homemade chocolate chip cookies from a cookie jar and brought them to the table.

"Help yourself," she urged. "Chipper, would you like some milk and cookies?"

The boy took less than an instant to make up his mind and abandoned a toy truck he had been rrr-rrr-ing across the blue and white linoleum. Jenny sat him at the table in his wooden highchair and placed a child's drinking cup before him. After she'd placed a cookie on the chair's tray, she sat across from Josh at the table, the boy between them.

She sipped her coffee and held the mug in both hands as if to warm them before she spoke.

Giving him a direct look, she asked, "First of all, how did you find us way out here, Josh?"

"Well, I flew into Bozeman last night," he explained, deliberately not mentioning the corporate jet, "and drove over to Turk in a rental this morning. When I got to Turk, I thought, now who would know where the Courter Ranch is? Then, I remembered Maybelle, the postmistress in Banjo. That's the little cowtown near my ranch. So I stopped in at the local post office. The lady there—Tillie, I believe—gave me directions."

He paused and took a large bite of another cookie.

Jenny smiled and agreed, "Yes, Tillie Ginn. She's a good friend of the family. Did she just come right out and give you directions?" she added curiously.

"Oh, no," Josh laughingly replied, "she gave me the once-over and asked some pointed questions. I knew I'd have to give her the whole story of how I knew Chris. I had a feeling she wouldn't send someone she didn't approve of out to the ranch."

"You're right there. She's a wonderful woman, very kind. You must have impressed her."

She smiled around the rim of her mug as she brought it to her lips.

"Maybe. I know I put my best foot forward," he managed to say.

A sad look passed over Jenny's pretty face, and she said, "I'm sorry that you missed the services after coming all this way. But, the a-accident was more than a month ago now." She paused and watched Chip devour his cookie and reach for another. She handed him one.

"Good, Jen-jen," the boy exclaimed with a big smile.

Jenny smiled lovingly in return.

"Yes, chocolate chips for Chip."

The little boy giggled at her words, and looked at Josh to see if he was laughing, too. He reached out to the man and said, "Dad-dy."

The room was very quiet for a moment before Jenny and Joshua regained their voices.

"No, Chip, not daddy." Jenny looked across the table at Josh, a plea in her expressive blue eyes. "He doesn't understand what's happened. He still asks for Chris and Sue. To Chip, you probably look a bit like him."

"No harm done. Chip, my name's Josh. Can you say that? Josh." He drew the word out, and Chip tried the unfamiliar word on his tongue.

"J-osssh," he imitated fairly well and waited for Josh's smile of approval.

"That's right, Chip! Good job." He reached over and patted the boy's silky blonde curls. He was reminded of the photo of Sue, Chip's mother, and the night he had first known of Jenny.

"Chris showed me a photo of Sue not long before he left the circuit and married her. Chip seems to have her curly blonde hair."

"Uh-huh," Jenny agreed. "And both Chris and Sue had blue eyes. Chip is named for Chris. Christopher John Courter, Junior. But Sue didn't want to call him Junior, and another Chris would lead to confusion, so they came up with Chip—as in 'a chip off the ole block'."

Jenny smiled easily across the table at him, and Josh returned the warm smile.

"Since Chris's hair was light brown, where did

you get your beautiful black hair, Jenny, if I may ask?"

"Oh, well, I take after my mother, I guess," she replied a little shyly. She felt her face warm when Josh said that her mother must have been a very pretty woman.

"She was, but she's been gone so long that sometimes it's hard to picture her. When that happens, I get out old photos. I never want to forget my parents, and I hope I can somehow help Chip to know his parents as real people . . . despite his being so young when they died." Jenny gripped her coffee mug tighter as she spoke, her determination coming through in her voice.

Josh looked steadily back at the young woman, his caramel eyes thoughtful. He admired her attitude, both toward the boy and his late parents. In fact, there were many things he admired about Jenny. Beautiful on the outside, but more importantly on the inside as well, Josh surmised.

"What will happen to Chip, Jenny? And while I'm asking, is there anything I can do to help?"

Surprised at his offer of help, she was at a loss for words. Then, gathering her thoughts, she replied,

"I'll raise Chip, of course, as I'm his only relative. We'll do just fine. I suppose the ranch will be his one day. In the meantime, I'll do everything I can to teach him how to care for it."

Josh shifted back in his chair.

"I admire your good intentions, Jenny. But what about your own life? What were you doing before the accident?"

For the first time since he'd appeared in her backyard, Jenny felt hostility toward her guest.

"It doesn't matter what I was doing," she said with an edge to her voice. "That can be put on hold for a few years. Chip is the most important person in my life right now, and I'll do my best for him. I know it may not always be easy. Shoot, it's not easy now, but it'll get better. The hurt over losing my brother and Sue will ease up gradually . . . I'm told."

Her tone said she wasn't too sure of that.

"Anyway, you've already helped by pushing old Bart Jones on his way today. I appreciate that very much," she continued, her voice warming a bit.

"I didn't mean to offend, Jenny."

A little wave of her hand said it was okay.

Jenny rose and went to the refrigerator. At the counter, she made a peanut butter and jelly sandwich for the boy's lunch and asked Joshua if he would care for anything.

"No, thanks, I'm fine, but I appreciate the offer," he replied.

After setting the sandwich before Chip, Jenny returned to her chair.

Josh went on, "What's his story, anyway? Bart, I mean. I saw the name on his pickup, so he must come from the ranch back down the road." He gestured with a jerk of his head in the direction he meant.

"Yes, he does. Would you like more coffee?" Jenny asked as she rose to take her empty mug for a refill. He did, so she filled both mugs before she sat back down.

"Good coffee," Josh commented, more to put Jenny at ease, as she seemed a bit agitated. Not one to lie, he did like the brew from the old blue-enameled pot.

"Thanks. It gets pretty strong by the end of the day. I like to keep a pot warming in case Zach stops by the house for a cup or two. But he likes it strong.

"Zach is our ranch foreman—has been for years, first with Dad, then with Chris. He's in his late sixties, I figure, but he's still spry and does a fine job. He lives in the bunkhouse. Cooks for himself mostly, though sometimes he gets to hankering for someone else's cooking, so when he hints I invite him to supper." She smiled fondly at the memory. "Sue did that, too, and Mom, years ago."

"Zach sounds like a good man, and a lucky one."

"He is," Jenny agreed. "Good, anyway. I'd trust

him with my life . . . though I don't think he can do it alone anymore. This is calving season, and in a few short months, we'll need to move the cows to summer grass. The ranch has grazing rights to pasture on the west slopes of the Madison Range. Herding the cows in the spring was easy enough for Chris, Zach and me. But with Sue gone . . . well, I'll have to watch Chip, and Zach can't do it alone. We'll have to look into hiring some drovers to get us through."

"Are they difficult to find? I suppose, like in Texas, some high school or college kids may want temporary work," Josh suggested.

"They won't be hard to find; the problem is pay . . ." she broke off mid-sentence. Jenny felt embarrassed at what she had almost let slip, and she ducked her head over her coffee mug. *No need to dump that little problem on him,* she thought.

Guessing at her true meaning, Josh relieved her anxiety by changing the subject.

"You were going to tell me about your neighbor," he prodded.

"Oh, yes," Jenny agreed, glad to talk about something else. "The valley holds just our ranch and his—High Meadows Ranch. It's always been that way, ever since my great-grandfather gave up looking for a gold strike and took claim to this spread. Bart's ancestors settled here about the same time. The families have gotten along pretty well over the years, but now Bart has gotten the idea that he and I should get married."

Why did that statement make him feel so angry? Josh's left hand curled into a fist under the table. He paid close attention to Jenny's story.

Chapter Four

"I guess the idea isn't so new, though, because Chris warned me about Bart. Apparently he'd hinted to Chris about marriage to me a few months ago. Chris and Dad didn't like Bart too much to begin with, and Chris would *never* have wanted me to marry him. I know *I* certainly don't want to."

She paused to wipe Chip's fingers and mouth. Then, she lifted the sturdy boy back to the floor, and he happily returned to his toy trucks.

Jenny sat back down at the table and took a sip of her coffee. The thick mug kept it warm, despite her talking more than drinking.

"Go on. I'm interested in hearing more."

"Well, to make it short, since the accident, Bart

has been stopping over everyday—to check on me and the boy, he says. It irritates me to no end," she exclaimed, "and I have trouble getting him to leave. That's what happened earlier today. Chip and I came back from town and found Bart waiting for us in his pickup."

Josh added, "I imagine he thinks he can wear you down, knowing you're on your own with Chip to care for."

"That's it I'm sure, but I'd never give in to *him*, the jerk! Why, he's old enough to be my father, and besides, I just don't like him," her voice rose as she emphasized her next words. "I think he's really trying to put our ranches together so *he* would end up owning the whole valley!"

Jenny banged her fist on the table in frustration.

"Most likely," Josh agreed with a frown creasing his forehead. "But don't sell yourself short. He may want your ranch, but getting *you* in the bargain must appeal to him, too."

Jenny flushed and couldn't meet his eyes for a few seconds.

Josh liked what he saw in this girl. *She's a real treasure.* His guts tightened at that realization. *Is Jenny the one I've been looking for? Now go slow, man, you don't want to spook her.*

He sat quietly for a moment as he sorted his thoughts, his facial expression sober. Then he looked intently at Jenny, his soft brown eyes caught and held her deep blue ones.

She felt her stomach clench. If she hadn't been already sitting down, she felt sure her knees would've wobbled. *My goodness! What's happening here?*

Josh cleared his throat and began to speak.

"Jenny, I want to be up front with you. It's been seven years since I'd last seen Chris, and while we'd been pals on the rodeo circuit, we hadn't kept in touch. He'd mentioned you to me. He loved you very much, you know."

Jenny had an odd expression on her lovely face. She wondered what Josh was getting at. Looking a bit misty, she said, "I know, and I loved him just as much. He was a wonderful big brother."

"The last time we talked, he told me about planning to marry Sue, but also about your father being ill and not having very long to live. When I saw that item in the paper reporting his and Sue's deaths, my first thought was that you were alone and might need some help. I made quick plans to fly up here, and I was nearly here before it dawned on me," Josh paused with am embarrassed grin, "that you were no longer a fourteen-year-old kid. That you could even be married, or in college, or out on your own somewhere. I felt foolish, but since I'd come this far, I decided to see it through.

So here I am, and I'd still like to help, if you'll let me."

Jenny's chin came up at a stubborn angle, and Josh thought she was about to send him packing.

"That—that's awfully kind of you, Josh. But I *am* grown up now. Besides, you can't stay long. I'm sure you have to get back to Texas soon."

Josh inserted quickly, "Eventually, but I set things up so I could be away for a while. Like Zach, I have a great foreman named Gabe Martinez who looks after the ranch for me. Consuela, his wife, is a wonderful cook and housekeeper. I'm lucky to have them."

"Do you have a family? Brothers and sisters? Are your folks alive? I don't mean to be nosy, Josh . . . I guess I'm just curious."

"No to all of your questions, Jenny. I haven't been lucky in that respect. My parents died in a plane crash about three years ago. I gave up my wild rodeo days then, and took over the business."

"I'm sorry about your parents, Josh. You've known loss, too. Perhaps that's what urged you to come to help." She seemed to be making a decision. "Well, maybe you can stay around for a week or so? Zach would welcome your help, I'm sure, and you obviously know ranch work already."

Josh flashed one of his handsome smiles in her

direction, and said, "Good, I'm glad that's settled. Is there a motel in Turk where I can stay?"

"No motels—there's a bed and breakfast, but you can stay here. I mean you can bunk with Zach." Her cheeks blushed, and she looked toward Chip playing on the floor. Taking a breath, she continued, "It's really very comfortable—small, but you can have your own bedroom."

Jenny suddenly laughed. It was the first time Josh had heard that lovely sound, and he felt it flow over and through him.

"What?" he asked, an answering smile playing about his lips.

"I just thought of a fringe benefit of your being here on the ranch—maybe Bart will finally get the hint that he's not welcome to come calling."

"Well, we'll have to make sure he takes that hint," Josh declared.

A short time later, Jenny put Chip down for his nap. When she was certain he was asleep, she and Josh walked down to the barns and found Zach in the tackroom mending a worn halter. Matthew lay nearby, his nose resting on his paws.

The older man glanced up and greeted Jenny as she stepped through the open door. He looked with curiosity at the tall cowboy who followed her into the room, then rose to his feet. The dog thumped his tail on the wooden floor.

Jenny gave Zach a warm smile, and said, "Hi, Zach. I want you to meet Chris's old friend who's come to see us all the way from Texas. Josh Brady, meet Zach Knutson, our foreman and my special friend."

With those words, she planted a quick kiss on the older man's grizzled cheek, and he grinned back at her. Zach gave his hands a quick swipe down his denim-covered thighs, before extending his hand to meet Josh's.

"Howdy, Josh Brady, glad to meet you," he said, while looking the younger man over.

Josh recognized that measuring look, and gave the man a firm handshake. "Glad to meet you, sir."

"Now where did you meet Chris, son?"

"We met rodeoing in college, and we rode the pro circuit together for a few years. He was a great guy . . . we had some good times together."

"Yep, I'd sure believe that. Chris was a humdinger. He liked his fun and jokes, but was a real hard-riding cowboy, too," the old man said, a mix of pride and sadness showing in his watery eyes.

"Zach, Josh has offered to spend a few days with us to give us both a hand. I figure you can find plenty for him to do to keep him busy." She flashed an impish grin at Josh.

"You bet, Jenny," Zach said. "I had a feeling

you ain't just a rodeo cowboy. Been working a ranch, too."

"All my life, Zach," Josh replied as he followed the others from the tackroom.

The three of them spent the next quarter hour walking through the barns while Zach kept up a running monologue about the running of the ranch. Josh could tell that Zach was as proud of the ranch operation as an owner would be.

Jenny added her views as well. She was pleased when Josh commented favorably on the quality of the Herefords, some of whom had come in to feed in the pasture.

When they returned to the barn Josh and Zach stopped to look over the horses. Jenny excused herself to go back to the house to check on Chip.

"I don't want to leave him alone in the house for more than a few minutes. Zach, please show Josh where he can bunk with you, and I'll gather the bedding."

"Will do, Jenny."

As she left the barn she invited both of them up to the house for supper.

"We'll eat early tonight, since we never had lunch today. Fried chicken okay?"

Zach heartily agreed, and Josh added, "Sounds great!"

* * *

The afternoon went by quickly much to Jenny's chagrin, as she had much she wanted to accomplish.

First, she laid out a plump pillow and sheets for the bunkbed, along with a warm blanket. She added an extra-long comforter in a brown and green plaid so that the extra-long cowboy would have enough cover. *He's one long drink of water,* she thought with a smile.

Before Chip woke up from his nap, Jenny put together an apple pie, taking a short-cut by using two frozen pie crusts from the big freezer on the backporch. *Sue would never have done that,* Jenny thought, *but she was a better baker than I am. Anyway, I'm in a hurry,* she added with a little toss of her brunette mane.

The heavenly aroma of the baking pie soon filled the kitchen, as Jenny peeled potatoes and covered the table with a blue linen cloth. Chip soon woke from his sleep.

"Mommy!" he called loudly from his bedroom upstairs. "Mommy!"

Jenny's heart jerked, and she dropped what she was doing and ran upstairs.

"Aunt Jenny's here, sweetheart," she said soothingly. The little boy stood in his crib, holding the top edge and bouncing up and down.

"Want Mommy!" he whimpered.

"I know, Chipper, but Mommy can't be here."

She lifted the wriggly boy out, and they visited the bathroom. Chip had been doing well with potty training, but the loss of his parents had unsettled him, and he was slow in getting back to his routine.

Jenny slipped him into a pair of tiny blue jeans and a fresh T-shirt with an MSU emblem on it that she had given him last Christmas.

They went down to the kitchen and Jenny set the table with her mother's china and blue water glasses. She and Zach didn't usually use her mother's china, but Josh was company and Jenny wanted to make his first meal on the ranch special.

When she heard a car door slam, Jenny nervously glanced out a window. Relieved that it wasn't Bart Jones coming back, she saw that it was Josh getting his luggage out of the Jeep. She told Chip about it in the habit she had developed of talking to him whenever they were alone in the kitchen. She thought it conducive to the development of his verbal skills.

"J-osssh," he babbled, drawing out the word as Josh had taught him earlier in the day.

"That's right, Chip. Josh is going to stay with us for awhile. Isn't that nice?"

"Yep, nice," he answered and pulled a book from a low shelf near his toybox. "Story, Jen-jen. Read story!"

"I'm busy now," she began, then changed her mind. "Okay, Chip. One story, then I'll have to cook our supper."

She moved to the rocker near his corner of the kitchen, sat down, and lifted the boy and his book onto her lap.

They were deep into the story of the little engine that thought it could when a knock sounded at the backporch door. The door opened, and Josh called her name.

"Come on in," she called back, and Josh stepped into the kitchen.

She didn't know what an appealing picture she and the boy made. Seeing Jenny in the rocker with Chip on her lap, Josh thought, *This is what I've been looking for, this is what I want.* He stopped short, his thoughts astonishing him, but thrilling him as well. He knew it was true.

Before he could say that he'd come up to the house for the blankets, he felt a sturdy little body tackle his leg. Chip had slid off Jenny's lap and run to him.

"Dad-dy! Dad-dy!" he squealed.

Josh, taken aback for just a moment, stooped to the boy's level and pulled him in for a hug.

"I'm Josh, Chip," he said in a choked voice as he dropped a kiss on top of the child's head.

Chip looked confused, but reached a tiny hand to Josh's cheek and patted it. "J-ossh?"

The man felt his heart turn over. He lifted his eyes to Jenny still in the rocker. She smiled rather sadly at him.

"This has been a hard day for him," she said by way of explanation. "He called for Sue when he woke up from his nap earlier. I think your height, your hat and maybe just your general appearance brings Chris to his mind."

She squeezed her eyes shut, trying to stop the tears that slid down her cheeks. As she impatiently dashed them away with her hands, Josh rose with Chip in his arms and walked to her. He put out a hand, and Jenny hesitated for a moment, then placed hers in his. He pulled her to her feet, put his left arm around her, drawing her into a circle with Chip and him.

Jenny gave a wavery sigh, and for just a moment let her head rest against his solid chest. The top of her head came just to his shoulder. His wonderful, strong shoulder that smelled of the fresh outdoors, and a clean-smelling aftershave.

Jenny gulped, pulled back a little, and said, "I'm sorry, Josh. I don't mean to cry, it's just that I love him so much, and it's so hard to see him wanting his—his parents." She deliberately didn't say mommy and daddy aloud, for fear of upsetting the boy again.

"No need to say sorry, Jenny. He's a fine little guy and would be very easy to love."

Chip reached toward his aunt, and she wrapped her free arm around him. He gave her a wet kiss on her left cheek. Josh grinned, leaned his head down and gave her a brief kiss on her right cheek.

"Oh !" Jenny breathed and looked up at Josh in surprise.

"Don't be upset—I just couldn't resist," Josh defended himself. Then, after a moment of looking deep into her wide blue eyes, he added, "I think you could use a break. It's been a difficult month for you, too. Zach tells me that you haven't been able to get out to the barns as you like to or to exercise the horses. Well, the first thing I'm going to do for you is to stay in the house tomorrow afternoon while you go out riding with your horse."

"Josh, that would be wonderful, but are you sure? Chip *can* be a handful," she warned.

Josh basked in the glow of her brilliant smile, before he answered.

"I'm sure. Hey, he'll be asleep the whole time, won't he?"

"Probably," Jenny replied with a chuckle, "but I'll show you where all his things are before I go out."

"Well, if you insist," Josh said with the air of a man who thought precautions were completely unnecessary.

Hmmm, thought Jenny, *this cowboy may be in for a rude awakening!*

Jenny slowed her Palomino mare, Ricci, to a walk once they had both had a good run. It had felt so good to both rider and horse to get out into the warm sunshine of late April and simply fly.

Now, Jenny opened her jacket, and they ambled along the top of a low ridge. It ran above a cold mountain stream that originated in the Madisons and flowed through the Courter spread. When they came to an outcropping of rock that afforded a view of the small valley, Jenny brought Ricci to a halt and dismounted to sit out on the rock. The mare contentedly nibbled at some early green shoots of grass that had pushed up in a small area devoid of snow.

The young woman shoved her hat back, pulled up her legs and hooked her arms around her knees. Matthew had run ahead of Jenny and the horse. Now he circled back and lay beside her on the rock shelf. They basked in the warmth of the sunshine beating down on the rock. It was a special spot to Jenny.

Growing up without a mother had made her adolescent years hard. Being the only female on the ranch, she often rode to this place when she wanted to be alone. It became easier for her once Sue came to live on the ranch, and Jenny learned to trust her. But there were still some things only Ricci heard. Today, just as during her adolescent years, Ricci was a wonderful listener. Quiet—but for the occasional snort—and non-judgmental.

Thinking aloud, Jenny told Ricci about the events of the past month, beginning with the tragedy of Chris and Sue's accident. She spoke about suddenly leaving college to care for her nephew, the kindness of friends, and the unexpected appearance of Josh Brady.

"I know everyone thinks I'm strong and willful, Ricci, but this has almost been more than I can handle. I'm worried that the county will try to take Chip away from me. I know Chris and Sue would want me to raise him, since I'm his only relative, but it's still there at the back of my mind.

"Then there's the concern about finances. Cash is dwindling fast. I'm praying there'll be enough to see us through 'til fall.

"I'm worried about Josh, too. It'd be so easy to lean on him, but he'll just be here for a short time, and I've got to plan for the long haul—keeping the ranch solvent, seeing that it's here for Chip when he grows up. Sometimes I'd like to just roll up in a ball and disappear. Isn't that silly, Ricci?"

The mare stamped one hoof and nodded her head as if in agreement.

Jenny laughed and dabbed her eyes with a tissue from her jacket pocket. She looked at Ricci.

"So, you think I'm silly, do you? No extra oats in *your* feedbag, old girl!"

Chapter Five

Jenny scrambled up from the rock and hugged the horse around the neck. Her voice muffled, she said, "To top it all off, I think I'm falling in love with him, but I've never been in love, so how would I know? Besides, I simply can't love him—he'll be gone before we know it. I'll have to guard against it, won't I, sweetie?"

She patted her mare lovingly and remounted. Taking her time, the horse walked back down the ridge to more even ground, and Jenny set her into an easy lope until they were within sight of the barn. After cooling her down, Jenny put her into her stall and curry-combed her. The brushing had a calming effect on Ricci, and the action always did the same for Jenny. She murmured soothing words of affection to her horse. Zach offered to clean Ricci's hooves while Jenny took Sue's gentle mare, Evie, for some exercise.

They made a few runs up and down the lane, then walked around the pasture for a while. Jenny turned Evie over to Zach since she had a feeling Chip was awake by now. She didn't want to try Josh's generosity, after he was so thoughtful to give her the gift of an afternoon off.

All was quiet when she walked into the kitchen. She went to the foot of the stairs and listened.

Nothing. Where's Josh?

Starting up the stairs, she heard a muffled splash and a squeal of delight from Chip. *The bathroom.*

The door was ajar, and Jenny paused. Josh was on his knees beside the tub. She knocked on the door, and he turned to her, a big grin on his face. His sleeves were rolled up exposing strong forearms. Rolling them up had done little good—most of his shirt was damp anyway. Chip was awash in a sea of bubbles and thoroughly enjoying himself.

Splashing Josh was obviously a lot of fun, Jenny observed.

"What's happening?" she asked pleasantly.

"Well, when Chip woke up, he had a dirty diaper. I figured this was the easiest way to get him clean again." He looked pretty proud of his handling of the situation.

"Looks like it worked," she agreed as Chip slapped both hands on the bubbly water again and chortled. "He's sure in a good mood."

"Yeah, it's been fun, but I'm not sure what to do next," Josh admitted.

"I'll take over then."

Jenny opened the drain to get rid of some of the bubbles, then rinsed Chip off.

For lack of a better place to sit, Josh sat on the lid of the stool and watched her.

Reaching out to tug the thick single braid that hung below her shoulders, he asked, "Did you have a nice ride?"

She answered, "Yes, it was lovely, thanks. Ricci and I both enjoyed it. I took Sue's mare Evie out, too, for a short run."

She lifted Chip from the tub and quickly wrapped him in a big fluffy towel.

Looking at Josh again, she said, "You're soaked. Why don't you go down the hall to Chris's closet and find a shirt that'll fit you. It's not as windy today, but you can't go out in a damp shirt."

He frowned. "Are you sure that's okay?"

"Yes, I wouldn't suggest it otherwise. Go ahead."

"I'm going." He headed out the door. "But

don't dress him yet. I want to see how you do it. I've never been around a baby before." His broad grin showed her he was enjoying it.

"Well, you're doing pretty well for no experience, cowboy." She gave him a warm smile. "It's the bedroom just across the hall from Chip's," she added, as she lifted Chip into her arms.

Josh paused just inside the bedroom. Feeling an intense sadness at the memory of how full of life Chris had once been, he looked around the room. Larger than Chip's, he surmised it had always been the master bedroom. Josh walked toward the closet. Beside it was a chest of drawers that held a wedding picture and a baby picture of Chip.

Opening the closet door and seeing the neatly hung clothing, for a moment he felt he was invading the couple's privacy. He selected a brown and tan Western shirt that he thought might fit. Luckily he and Chris were close in size.

As he came into the nursery he saw Jenny changing Chip. "Now, how do you put one of these contraptions on?" he asked, eyeing the disposable diaper Jenny had picked up.

"It's simple really. Just watch."

Josh admired her deftness as Jenny diapered Chip.

She slipped on the boy's little jeans and a warm pull-over. She let Josh put on his clean socks. He was all thumbs at first, complaining that they were so small, but he eventually got the job done. The sneakers went on a little easier, and Chip was dressed.

Carrying the boy, Josh followed Jenny downstairs. Setting Chip on his feet, he watched him head toward the kitchen with his aunt not far behind.

"Say, Jenny, may I use your phone? I'll put it on my card. I need to check in with Emily, let her know how long I may be gone."

Jenny stopped in her tracks. *Emily? Who's Emily?* she wondered with a thump of her heart. *Is he married or engaged and hasn't told me—us?* she amended quickly.

But she turned and, in a calm voice replied "Of course. Feel free to use the one in the ranch office." She directed him to the room off the hall that Chris and her father had used for that purpose.

"Thanks, I won't be long."

"Take your time," she said rather coolly and hurried away toward the kitchen.

Josh just grinned. *She sounded jealous*, he thought with satisfaction.

He entered the room Jenny had pointed out and looked around. A large walnut desk dominated the room. A deep-green leather couch, a few chairs, a file cabinet, and bookshelves completed the furnishings.

Josh's eye was drawn to a shelf that held several plaques, trophies and ribbons that attested to Chris's prowess as a horseman and to the excellence of the Courters' Hereford stock. In a prominent spot was his belt buckle from Nationals. *Someday I'll have to tell Chip about that particular rodeo. I want him to be proud of his old man.*

Moving to the desk, Josh called his secretary, and when the switchboard at Starr Enterprises connected him to her office, he greeted her warmly.

"Hi, Em! It's me. Thought I'd better check in with you. What's been happening?"

He sat down in the desk chair while he listened to Emily's rundown of the last two days, gave her his opinion on a few matters, and answered her question about how long he'd be gone.

"At least another week, Em. Things are a little complicated here, and there are some things I can do to help Jenny's situation. Besides, I'm having a great time. I actually gave the little boy a bath today. Can you believe it?"

Smiling broadly at Emily's surprise, he joined her in laughter. "Yeah, I know. Absolutely no experience, but I'm learning."

After a few more minutes, he told Emily that he'd call again on Friday, but that if she needed to talk to him sooner to call him. He gave her the ranch's phone number.

"One more thing, Em. I may bring home a surprise. No, I'm not going to tell you now, but it involves something you've been after me about."

With a chuckle, he hung up. He leaned back in the chair, rested his clasped hands behind his head, and smiled the smile of a contented man.

In the kitchen, Jenny muttered to herself as she measured and stirred the ingredients for biscuits to accompany the beef stew she had put into a crock pot that morning. It smelled wonderful, but Jenny didn't notice. She dumped the dough onto a pastry board and proceeded to punch the daylights out of it.

Emily! she thought. *Darn, drat, fiddlesticks!*

The second part of Josh's plan to give Jenny a break from her troubles was to suggest that they go out to dinner by themselves on Saturday night.

He mentioned it after Wednesday evening's beef stew and biscuits.

Zach went back to the bunkhouse after supper, and Josh offered to dry the dishes while Jenny washed.

Jenny stopped washing the plate in her hand when he asked her to dinner, then laid the plate back in the sudsy water. Her back to Josh, she said, "I don't know, Josh. I'll have to think about it. Going out by ourselves sounds a lot like a—a date, and we probably shouldn't be doing that."

There, I handled that okay. I'll remember Emily, even if he doesn't, she thought with a self-satisfied sniff.

"Oh, well, we don't have to call it a *date*," Josh put in quickly, priding himself on thinking fast before she said a definite no. His voice casual, as if her answer was of no importance to him he added, "Besides, most people would think I'm too old for you. You're what—twenty-one? Twenty-two?"

Still not looking at him, she kept her hands in the water as she spoke. "Twenty-one, last October. H-how old are you?"

"Thirty-one, last October, too. Say, when is your birthday?"

When she said it was the twenty-third, he whooped, "How about that! Mine's the twenty-fourth!"

"Really?" Jenny cried as she turned to face him, her hands dripping sudsy water.

Josh handed her the dishtowel to dry them on.

"Really. We're practically twins—that is, if you ignore the ten years between us," he added with a rueful smile. "Anyway, I just wanted to give you a break from being responsible all the time. Is there someone you could ask to babysit for you?"

"Well, I suppose so," she admitted. "But,

but . . ." *Oh, shoot, I might as well just come right out and ask him.* "Josh, are you married or engaged or anything?"

Her cheeks grew warm as she waited for his reply. He looked so surprised, she thought he wouldn't answer. Thinking she had overstepped some male boundary, she turned back to the sink.

"I'm sorry," she mumbled, "it's really not my business."

Josh said, "No, Jenny, it's okay." He leaned against the counter and continued. "No, I'm not married, never have been. Not engaged either, though I almost was, once. Her name was Dawn. She was a girl that I met in college. But I came to my senses in time to realize that a city girl is not for me. I've had a few girlfriends over the years, but there's no one special in my life."

He almost added, *Except for you, Jenny.*

Jenny turned to him. Her eyes flashed blue sparks as she demanded, "Then who the heck is Emily?"

"Oh, is *that* what's been bothering you tonight?" Josh asked with a laugh.

That really did it. She snorted in anger, then turned and rushed from the kitchen and up the stairs to her room. The slam of the door reverberated through the house.

"Ouch!" Josh said to Chip who looked at him,

his little mouth pursed in an O. "It's okay, Chip, *I'm* the one in trouble."

Chip went back to knocking over and re-stacking his blocks, and Josh scrubbed out the crock pot that was the only piece left in the sink.

Upstairs, after the satisfying slam of the door, Jenny threw herself on the bed, rolled over to her back and hugged a pillow to her chest. *What's the matter with me? I can't believe I just ran out on Chip. What kind of mother am I going to make? All because I got jealous of someone named Emily that I know nothing about. Good heavens, now I have to go back and face Josh.* She threw the pillow aside and sat up. Serves me right for losing my temper.

A few minutes later, Jenny returned to the kitchen. Looking sheepish, she apologized to Josh.

"I'm sorry, Josh. I have a lousy temper some-times. I shouldn't have run out on you and the dishes, and especially Chip."

"You don't have a lousy temper, you have a very healthy temper." Josh grinned at her. "And I apologize, too, because I provoked it."

Shaking her head, she protested, "But I was so rude—and you're being so nice!"

He walked over to her, took her slender shoulders in his big hands, and held her eyes with his. "I should've told you immediately who Emily is," he said seriously. "She's my secretary at the business I run in Dallas. She was my father's secretary before me. She's in her fifties, and she and her husband have four grandkids. Em's a wonderful gal, and I couldn't have survived these past three years without her. When Dad died, I had to take over his business earlier than I wanted and her support really helped."

Having spoken his piece, he continued looking deeply into her wide blue eyes. *I'd better let go before I do something dumb*, he thought, at the same moment his lips met hers.

His words registered with Jenny, because as she watched his eyes change from caramel to deep brown, she felt a little burst of gratitude that Emily was a grandmother. Then, his lips touched hers.

She looked mesmerized. Her face was flushed, and her eyes were a dark blue and decidedly dazed.

Usually not at a loss for words, she barely got out a whispered, "Wow!"

"Yeah, me too!" Josh agreed with a grin. "Come to think of it, I *do* want Saturday dinner to be a date. What do you say?"

"Y-yes," Jenny replied, returning his smile.

"Good. I suppose I should get down to the bunkhouse—I told Zach I'd play checkers with him this evening. Will you and Chip be all right?"

"Of course. Almost bedtime for him," she

stated, as she looked over at the little boy caught in the midst of a big yawn.

"Goodnight, Chip," Josh said and walked to the back porch. He shrugged on his jacket and grabbed his Stetson, then turned to Jenny.

" 'Night, Jenny," he whispered.

"Goodnight, Josh."

Long after she had read Chip a story and tucked him into his crib, she lay awake in the room that had been hers all her life. She re-played every moment she had spent with Josh, every word he'd spoken, and wondered exactly when she had fallen for him.

So much for guarding against falling for him. She rolled over in bed, plumped her pillow, and closed her eyes. Her last conscious thought before falling asleep was that he'd be going back to Texas soon. *There was really no chance of this attraction going anywhere, anyway. Life just wasn't fair sometimes.*

Down in the bunkhouse, Zach and Josh enjoyed a few competitive checker games along with coffee and conversation.

"You're killing me, Zach!" Josh complained good-naturedly.

"Haw, boy, I am, ain't I?" he said teasingly. "I've played a lot of games in my time. Jenny's dad and I kept a running tournament going for years. Chris played some, but Jenny's real good . . . she used to come down most evenings for a game or two."

He paused while he studied the board, then moved a piece out of Josh's path with finesse.

" 'Course, the last few years she hasn't been home as much, what with goin' to college and all."

Josh looked up from the checkerboard. "Jenny's going to college? She hasn't mentioned that."

"Yep, for three years now. She's been studying over at Bozeman. 'Course, she stayed home after the accident. Couldn't leave the boy."

"What was she studying?" Josh asked, wanting to learn as much about Jenny as he could.

"Wants to be a teacher. Little kids, I guess. It figures, though. Jenny always wished she had lots of brothers and sisters," the older man replied.

"I can picture that," Josh said musingly. "She's awfully good with Chip."

"She sure loves that little tyke," Zach put in. Then, "King me!"

Chapter Six

"Hey!" Josh hollered, "I got distracted by you talkin' about Jenny."

Zach leaned back from the table with a twinkle in his eyes. "You like our Jen, Josh?"

Josh leaned back as well and looked at Zach for a moment, before he said with a grin, "Does it show?"

"I think so. I see it, anyway," Zach replied. "How does she look to you?"

"I don't know, Zach. I know she's been through a lot lately, so I don't want to rush her into anything. To tell you the truth, Chris showed me her picture years ago. She was just a kid, about fourteen, but there was something about her—her eyes, I think—that just got to me.

"Then I did something sort of foolish," he admitted. "When I read in the Dallas paper that Chris and Sue had been killed, I immediately headed for Bozeman thinking little Jenny might need some help. I was almost here before it dawned on me that she wasn't fourteen anymore. She was grown—maybe even married or something."

He ran his fingers through his hair, then rested his forearms on the table.

"When I got to Turk, Tillie at the post office told me how to find the ranch," Josh continued, but noted how Zach's eyes lit up at the mention of Tillie. "Do you know Tillie? Of course you do, everyone knows everybody else in a small town. Anyhow, they sure do in my part of Texas!" Josh laughed at the thought.

"Yeah," Zach admitted, "she's a good ol' girl. I think about asking her out to supper sometimes, but I just never do it. Coward, I guess."

"Well, you should, Zach. Life goes by too fast. You should reach for what you want and hold on."

A look of sadness crossed the old man's face. "I did that once, but I wasn't able to hold on."

"What do you mean?" Josh asked curiously.

"It's been over forty years, now. I came back to Montana after doing a few years in the Navy during the war—the Korean War, that is—and I'd saved a bit of money. I found a nice piece of land up near the Big Belts that a man could work, with the help of a good woman."

He paused to collect his thoughts and to settle his emotions.

"I found her, too. Mattie was the younger sister of a fellow I'd worked with before I'd left for the service. She was a tiny thing, pretty as a peach, but a hard worker, too. We took to each other right off, and got married a couple months later. It was tough going, but we kept at it, and our little place began to look like home."

He paused again and swallowed a gulp of coffee.

Josh urged him to continue. "What happened, Zach?"

"Well, Mattie wanted more than anything to have a family, and she fretted about it 'til finally, about three years later, she got pregnant. She was tickled pink, and I was damn proud myself. But I guess Mattie just wasn't meant to be a mother. She started labor early, and even though I got a neighbor lady to come and help her, it was too late."

Josh sighed, "Did she die, Zach?"

"Yeah," he answered, and Josh reached across the checkerboard to grip his forearm.

"The boy, too," he added. "Doc said she was just too tiny and couldn't do it on her own. If she'd been in a city where there was a hospital, maybe . . . but no matter now. It was a long time ago."

"I'm sorry, Zach," his friend said in sympathy. "What did you do then?"

"I stayed on for awhile, but I didn't have the heart for it. A year or so later, I ran into Jenny's dad at a cattle auction in Lewistown. I'd known him for years, even cowboyed here for him for a spell before the Navy. He said he was lookin' for a good man to work his land and offered the job to me. I went back home and sold my place to a neighbor and I've been here ever since.

"So, I'm too old and set in my ways to want to start up with a woman again. But you, boy, should take your own advice. If you want Jenny, hang in there."

"I will. She's what I've been looking for these last few years. I may have to live in the city part of the time because of running my parents' business, but I want to marry a girl who loves ranching as much as I do. Besides," he added with a devilish grin, "when I first saw her, just yesterday mornin', she 'bout knocked my socks off!"

"Yep, she's a purty one, all right."

After a few minutes of companionable silence, each man lost in his own thoughts, Josh brought up finances. He explained to Zach about the corporation he had inherited, and the Texas ranch. He asked about what the Courter Ranch was facing with Chris gone, and Zach answered his questions honestly.

Zach added, "Jenny has a lot of pride, Josh. She's a strong girl and kinda stubborn. But I know she's worried. A social worker came out a few days after the funerals—Chip being an orphan and all—and asked a lot of questions. They let Chip stay with Jenny, but the will hasn't been read yet. I think that comes up next Tuesday. I know she's counting on that to make her Chip's permanent guardian.

"As far as cash goes, that's tight right now. Even the life insurance and truck insurance have been held up. A lot hangs on what Chris and Sue said in their wills," he said with a shake of his head. "The waiting's hard on the girl, but she'd likely not admit it."

"I agree with you about that," Josh commented. "Well, I know what I *want* to do. Now, I've just got to figure out a way to do it without getting Jenny riled. Say, do you ever babysit Chip? I want to take Jen out to supper Saturday night, just the two of us."

"Why sure, boy. Can't say I've ever done it, but by golly, I'll muddle through."

The next day, Jenny took Chip into Turk for a play session with his little friends at Beth's daycare center. While he was there, she followed her usual routine and stopped by the post office.

Tillie was full of questions about the good-looking Texas cowboy she'd sent out to the Courter place. When she heard Jenny's answers, Tillie was satisfied that her hunch was right. Josh Brady may well be that miracle she'd prayed for. For one thing, Jenny was more like her old lively self, and Tillie soon found at least part of the reason why.

Jenny asked, "Tillie, I'm hoping you can babysit Chip for me Saturday evening. Josh asked me out to supper—just the two of us. What do you think?"

"Why, sure, Jen, I'd be happy to. A real date, huh? Fast worker that fellow, but then I'd expect nothing less from a handsome Texan!" Tillie exclaimed with what could only be described as a belly laugh.

Jenny laughed, too, and remarked, "He is sort of handsome, isn't he?"

"Do you know where he plans to take you? Since he's new around here, maybe you should pick the place. And when do you want me to come out?" Tillie asked, quite pleased with this turn of events.

"Would six o'clock be okay? Maybe I'll suggest going to the Narrows," referring to a stone house along the river that had been converted into a restaurant, "or, if he wants to drive that far, over to Bozeman."

"Now you wear something pretty that you can dance in, Jenny. I'll bet he's danced a Texas two-step in his time," Tillie suggested with a conspirative twinkle in her eyes.

"I will, Tillie. That sounds like fun," she added with a grin. "Thanks. I'll look for you about six, then. I hope you don't mind driving out to the ranch?"

"Heavens, no. It'll be easier for Chip that way, and you won't have to drag his things into town. Now, you run along, and just think about having a good time." She shooed Jenny toward the door with a wave of her hands.

"Bye, Tillie."

Zach and Josh had eaten breakfast at the bunkhouse that morning, as they wanted to get an early start on some fence mending. A job that needed to get done, and one that would be easier working together.

Jenny and Chip had slept a bit later than usual. She had fed Chip his breakfast, but with the men somewhere out in the pastures, she wanted to leave the house before Bart had a chance to stop by.

Now that more than an hour had passed, she felt hungry and stopped at the Cowboy Cafe for coffee and a donut. She slipped into a booth, took a bite of a yummy chocolate-covered pastry, and sighed in satisfaction. But, as luck would have it, the door opened and Bart Jones came in.

Oh, no, she thought, and looked away, hoping he hadn't seen her. But he zeroed in on her and strode straight to her booth.

"Howdy, Jen. Thought I saw you come in here."

He made a move to sit opposite her, and she indicated she was about to leave.

"Oh, you just got here. Finish your coffee, at least," Bart told her, as he sat down. "I want to talk to you."

"We don't have anything to say to each other, Bart. You're a good neighbor, but I'm not interested in anything else," Jenny answered in a firm voice. She was determined to hold her own.

His air of friendliness vanished. "I'll bet if I was that Texas cowboy, you'd sit and talk to me," he declared with a sneer. "I saw the way he looked at you. Been having to fight him off, Jen? Or maybe you don't *want* to fight him off."

Her head snapped up, and anger, blazing, white-hot anger, flashed through her veins. She pinned Bart with a look that said she thought him lower than the lowest snake.

"Just shut your mouth, Bart Jones. You don't know anything about him, or me either, for that matter. Now, get away from this table. I don't want you near me!"

Jenny's voice carried, and she flushed when she realized the other patrons were staring her way. George, the cafe's owner, came over.

"Trouble, Jenny?" he asked pleasantly, giving Bart a level look.

Bart got up disgruntledly, looked at George angrily, and said to Jenny, "This ain't done yet. You'd better watch yourself, or you just might be real sorry!"

With those words, he stormed out of the small cafe.

Jenny paid her bill, thanked George for his concern, and left—but not before checking that Bart wasn't lurking outside.

Over the next two days, Jenny kept secret her encounter with Bart. After all, he couldn't *make* her marry him, she decided, so there was no reason to take his warning seriously.

On Saturday, she gave Chip his supper a little early, and took him upstairs with her while she prepared for her date. When they went back downstairs, Zach and Josh were in the kitchen.

Jenny thought Josh looked wonderful in a brown Western-cut suit worn with a yellow shirt. He carried a tan Stetson and wore snakeskin boots. But Jenny was surprised to see Zach coming up to the house with him, in good jeans and a neatly pressed blue plaid shirt.

"What's up, guys?"

"Josh, here, asked me to babysit the boy, Jenny. I hope that's okay," the older man said uncertainly.

"That's real thoughtful of you, Zach, thanks. But I asked someone to sit tonight, too!" She gave Josh a puzzled look. "I didn't know you'd made plans with Zach. Anyway, Tillie will be here around six to watch Chip."

Josh was noticing how pretty Jenny looked in a green flared skirt and a silky cream blouse. His caramel eyes traveled down to her tan boots and back up again. He suddenly heard what she was saying, and turned to Zach.

"Say, that'll make it more fun and easier, too, Zach. Tillie and you can handle Chip together." The wink he gave the man reminded him of what he'd said about Tillie during the checker game.

Why, Zach is actually blushing, Jenny observed. *Hmmm, something's going on here.*

They heard a car pull up, and Tillie arrived, looking her usual casual-but-neat self in comfortable jeans and a maroon crewneck sweater.

She greeted everyone warmly and, though Zach offered to retreat to the bunkhouse, she said she'd be pleased to have his company for the evening.

Jenny showed Tillie where everything was and

told her and Zach to help themselves to the cherry pie in the cupboard. Before long, she and Josh were leaving in his rented Jeep. Jenny had suggested that since they were dressed up, they drive out to Bozeman to the Narrows Restaurant.

"The food's good and it's very nice. If we eat in Turk, the choice is pretty limited."

"Then the Narrows it is," Josh agreed. "You look so pretty tonight, I want to take you someplace nice and show you off." He gave her a grin, then looked back at the road.

"You look kinda handsome tonight yourself, cowboy," she replied, teasing him a little.

He reached out with his right hand and caught her left hand in a quick squeeze.

A half hour later, they were seated in an alcove table near a window that afforded a view across the river to the mountains beyond. As they looked over the menu, Josh remarked that they should come here again when the weather was warmer, and they could sit out on the deck.

"That'd be nice," Jenny agreed, then looked back at her menu. *He's thinking of another time?* she puzzled. *But he's going back to Texas.*

When their dinners had been served—a salmon steak with a potato and salad for Josh, and grilled trout with fettuccine for Jenny—they chatted while they ate. A pianist seated to one side of a huge stone fireplace provided pleasant background music.

Jenny enjoyed hearing Josh's tales about growing up on a Texas ranch; and, in particular, his and Chris's adventures on the rodeo circuit.

"I've never heard any of this, Josh. But that's probably because I'm twelve years younger than Chris, and he thought I was too young to hear about his shenanigans," she said between giggles at their exploits. Wiping tears of laughter from her eyes with a tissue from her shoulder bag, she urged him to continue.

"Not much else to tell, Jen. I just want you to know that I thought Chris was a good man, and I'm proud to have been his friend."

She looked across the small table at him. A sense of wonderment came over her that this man had so suddenly come into her life. *I'm so fortunate!*

Josh looked back and wondered what she was thinking. She looked lovely tonight. The cream blouse looked demure with its long sleeves and ruffles at the wrists and throat, but the silky material complemented her slender figure. The skinny girl had matured nicely. She wore her ebony hair up in a chignon. Josh thought it made her look older and more sophisticated . . . but it only made him want to take it down and run his hands through her hair.

He cleared his throat and said, "Your turn, Jenny. I've been doing all the talking. Tell me what life was like for you as a girl."

She smiled gently, and replied, "Well, not much different than yours, I suppose. School, church, 4-H club, helping with the chores. I've always loved the ranch—caring for the calves and horses. Dad gave me my own horse when I was twelve, though Chris had taught me to ride years before. To me, pure happiness is getting on Ricci's back and riding out over the ranch. Ricci loves it, too."

"She has good lines. Do you ever take her to horse shows?" Josh asked.

"Yes, several times over the years, and we do very well."

Josh smiled at her enthusiasm. Most of the women he'd dated had no interest in ranch life or horses. *But no city airs about this girl, she's completely natural. Definitely my kind of woman.*

Aloud he said, "will you be going to the upcoming show in Wild Rose?"

"Yes, we are. Gosh, that's next month. I'd nearly forgotten with all that's happened, but it's on the calendar in the office. Oh, thanks for helping me think of it," she replied, her gratitude showing plainly. "That may mean some cash for the ranch operation."

"Good, I'm glad. Do you have your own horse trailer?"

"Yes, we do, but . . ." she paused, frowning slightly, as she laid her linen napkin beside her plate. "I think I'll have to make other arrangements this year . . . there's no pickup to *pull* the horse trailer."

Josh saw her look of distress and made a quick decision.

"We'll take care of that on Monday. Zach mentioned that the insurance money to replace the ranch's pickup hadn't been released yet."

Jenny immediately protested, raising her hands as if to halt him. "I can't let you go to that expense, Josh, we'll just wait for . . ."

"No, it's no trouble for me to replace the truck, and Zach needs it for everyday work, right?" She nodded, but Josh saw that her pride was hurt. "Now, honey, just give in graciously, because I *am* going to get you a truck on Monday. You come along and make the decision as to what you want."

As he talked, he reached across the table and took her left hand in his right and held it. Looking at her dainty but sturdy hand, then at the stubborn look on her face, he added, "If it'll make you feel better, you can pay me back out of the insurance settlement." Her face softened and her hand relaxed in his.

"Of course," he continued with a twinkle in his eyes, "you don't *have* to pay me back. Thanks to my family's hard work I'm very comfortable monetarily. And, I've been lucky enough to keep the ranch holdings and Starr Enterprises secure since I took over. Besides, you're Chris's little sister, and as I said before, I *want* to help."

He saw a fleeting look of disappointment on her face before she withdrew her hand. What had he said wrong?

She forced a bright smile, and said, "Thank you for your kindness, Josh, but I *will* pay you back when I'm able. I'm grateful for the help you've given me and Zach these past few days, but I can't become dependent on you or your generosity."

He looked hurt at her words, but quickly erased any evidence of that from his face. Jenny wondered why he should be upset. After all, she was only trying to be adult about her new responsibilities, and she didn't want to accept money from anyone.

He only asked, "Would you care for dessert?"

Jenny felt oddly let down. *He wants to end our date and leave.*

"I don't think so, but you go ahead, if you'd like some."

"No," he answered distractedly. *Is she anxious to get out of here? I haven't handled this very well.*

Josh signaled for the check, and Jenny took his

offered arm as they exited the restaurant and walked to the Jeep.

Not wanting the evening to end so abruptly despite Jenny's sudden coolness, Josh asked her if she'd like to go for a drive.

"Perhaps take a look around Bozeman?" he suggested and hoped she'd agree. What he really wanted was a chance to hold her in his arms again, and maybe find a place to go dancing. That'd do it.

Chapter Seven

By the time they reached Bozeman, their conversation was on comfortable ground again. Feeling more sure of himself, he asked if she knew of any dance spots.

She replied with a little laugh, "Tillie said I should take you dancing. She said a good ole Texas cowboy'd dance a two-step a time or two."

His answering laugh confirmed that. "Yep, I do like to dance," he drawled in his best Texas accent.

"Well, Lindhaus Tavern puts on Saturday evening dances . . . we could stop by there." Her voice betrayed her eagerness, and Josh was happy to hear it.

The tavern was crowded, but Josh took Jenny's

hand and skirted the large dance floor. He sat her at a small table off to one side, helped her off with her jacket, and tossed his Stetson on the table.

Offering to get her something to drink, she opted for a cola. He came back with her soda and an alcohol-free beer for himself, since he was driving back to Turk later. Jenny appreciated his carefulness.

As the music changed, they went to the dance floor to try that two-step Tillie had mentioned. Jenny quickly caught on to the steps that Josh led her through. It was fun. A lead dancer taught a line dance, and they found themselves doing lively steps to the song of a young country-and-western star.

Jenny was enjoying herself, and she hoped Josh was, too. When a slower tune came on, he took her into his arms. She felt happy there, and he pulled her close and laid his cheek on her soft hair.

She gave a sigh of contentment. She could feel his strong heartbeat where he held her hand against his chest. The song playing was "Make the World Go Away", and Jenny gave in to the music. Josh truly did make the cares of her world go away, if just for the length of the song.

When it ended, they returned to their table. It was too noisy to really talk, so they contented themselves with watching the other dancers and sipping their drinks. When she checked her watch and saw that it was nearly ten o'clock, she suggested that they head back soon. Josh agreed, but insisted on one more dance.

"Who knows, we may never get a chance to dance again, and I like holding you in my arms," he whispered in her ear, once they were on the dance floor.

She looked up at him, unaware that her heart was showing in her eyes. After all, she was a novice at being in love, and whispered back, "It feels nice being here."

Josh couldn't help himself. He ducked his head and pressed a gentle kiss to her sweet lips. When he broke the kiss, she smiled at him and lifted her left hand to caress his jaw. His answering smile thrilled her to her toes, and he pulled her even closer.

Neither said anything more until they were on their way back to Turk. Earlier Jenny had avoided looking at the spot where Chris had gone off the highway, but now she felt compelled to show Josh. With her hands clasped tightly in her lap, she pointed it out.

"It was right along here where the pickup went off the road," she said quietly. "The highway patrolman thinks Chris must have braked suddenly—possibly for an animal as there were fresh deer tracks in the snow—and lost control on the ice. They think he started off on the right side, over-corrected, and skidded off into the river. The pickup rolled down the bank and landed upside down in the water." Her voice broke, and she swallowed hard.

"You don't have to talk about it, honey," Josh assured her as he patted her hands, still clenched in her lap.

"I—I think I want to. I haven't talked to any-one, even Zach. He was hurting too much him-self." She opened her hands; Josh slowed the vehicle and held them in his, as she continued to talk. "The coroner said Sue died on impact, and Chris a few minutes later. If he had lived he would've been paralyzed . . . his neck was bro-ken."

Tears streamed down her cheeks as she talked, and she dashed them away with her free hand, and took a shaky breath.

"That would've been tough on Chris," Josh commented. In his mind, he was seeing Chris not able to ride, to teach his son, to pull his own weight around the ranch. Yes, Chris would've hated that. But he would have been alive.

Josh's thoughts were drawn back to Jenny as she went on.

"I feel so guilty sometimes. I'd been staying in Bozeman during the week, but almost always drove home for weekends. That's what I'd done that weekend. Their anniversary was coming up on Monday, and I offered to baby sit Chip on Saturday night so they could go out. They decided to drive to Bozeman for dinner and a movie. If I hadn't come home that weekend, they wouldn't have been out on the road."

She snuffled and gulped back a sob. Josh held her hand tightly to emphasize his words.

"Jenny, don't blame yourself. It wasn't your fault at all. It was just an accident that could have happened anytime on any icy road, no matter where they were."

"In my mind I know that's true, but I can't accept it. One thing though, it happened on their way back home. At least they'd had their romantic anniversary dinner."

"That's a good memory to keep, Jenny. They had a nice evening celebrating their anniversary," he said encouragingly.

"But I miss Chris terribly, and Sue. She was such a sweetheart. I wasn't sure about her when they first married—I was barely fifteen and thought I didn't need anyone to mother me. But Sue didn't force anything. She just treated me like a sister, and we got along really well. She helped me through those awkward teen years, you know, like how to handle boys and all those other issues."

Josh pulled the Jeep into a scenic look-out. This was too important, and he wanted to give her his full attention. He unbuckled his seatbelt and shifted toward her.

"What would she have thought about me?" he asked.

Jenny pulled a handkerchief from her shoulder bag and wiped her face. As he stroked her damp cheek with the back of his hand, she turned toward him.

"I—I'm not sure. You're different from any other guy I've dated. Well, I haven't quite figured you out yet, but I think Sue would've liked you."

She lowered her gaze when he asked, "Do *you* like me?"

She felt as if she couldn't get her breath, but whispered, "Yes, I do."

Josh said that he was glad because he liked her, too. He laid his hat on the dashboard and placed his right hand on the nape of her neck, while he tipped her chin to him with his left.

He kissed her, and Jenny slipped her arms around him and returned his kisses with all the emotion in her young heart. A passing car startled them. He took a deep breath and said, "We'd better head back."

She agreed, "Yes, we should get home," and sat back into her seat and buckled up. She was very quiet the rest of the drive to the ranch.

Josh wondered what she was thinking about, afraid that her silence bode no good for him.

Jenny wondered if she had seemed too enthusiastic. Heaven knows, she didn't want him to think she was throwing herself at him.

All was well at the ranch when they arrived. Tillie and Zach were just finishing another checker game at the kitchen table.

Jenny looked at Josh and smiled. Over dinner he had told her of Zach's interest in Tillie. It seemed the older couple had enjoyed their evening together.

With a big smile, Tillie asked if they'd had a nice time. She was delighted that they'd gone dancing. "I knew you'd like to dance, Josh, the first time I laid eyes on you," she added.

Josh just grinned back at her.

"Did Chip give you a hard time?" Jenny asked, hoping the answer was no.

"Oh, we had a good ole time," Zach replied. "Tillie read to him, and I got these old bones down on the floor for some first class truck racin'."

Tillie laughed. "He was real good, Jen. Settled down to sleep like a little angel."

"Good," Jenny said, relieved that Chip had been on his best behavior.

Tillie got ready to leave. She turned down Josh's offer to follow her home.

"Oh, my goodness, that's not necessary."

"At least call me when you get there," Jenny asked and gave Tillie a hug of thanks.

"I'll do that, just to make you happy," Tillie agreed, giving the young woman's cheek a soft pat.

Zach gathered his checker game and walked Tillie to her car, then went on to the bunkhouse. Jenny and Josh were left alone in the kitchen.

Jenny removed her jacket and laid it over a chair.

"Would you like coffee, Josh?" she offered, going to the pot and checking if there was any left.

"No coffee, Jen, but I would like to stay until Tillie calls, just to be sure she's home safe. Anyway, there's a lot more I want to talk to you about."

"Oh, there is?" she asked, as she turned from the stove. Josh was sitting in the chair Zach had just vacated. She took the one opposite him and clasped her hands under the table.

He looked soberly at her, which only served to make her more nervous.

"I want to . . ." he began.

"Josh, I . . ." she said at the same time. Then, "You go ahead."

"Okay. Well, I think I handled our conversation at the restaurant badly. Maybe left you with the wrong impression. I didn't purposely flaunt my wealth, but I'd be very happy to use my resources to help you and Zach get through this hard time."

"You didn't offend me, Josh," she interrupted, "I'm just trying to stand on my own." She bit her lower lip and looked tense.

Josh got up and circled the table to stand behind her chair. He placed his hands on her shoulders. "I admire you for that, Jen, but it's okay to accept help sometimes. You know that I came here because you're Chris's little sister, but as soon as I saw you, that changed. I knew that wasn't the reason I wanted to stay."

His fingers massaged her neck and shoulders, and she soon began to relax. "It wasn't?" she asked, a quaver in her soft voice.

"No, it wasn't," he replied, as he began to take the hairpins out of the loose bun she'd worn for their date. "What do you call this thing, anyway?"

"What? My hairdo? It's just a twist, I guess. Nothing special. Why?"

"It looks very nice, but I think I like it down long best," he said, as he ran his fingers through the thick waves that now hung to the middle of her back.

Getting up quickly, she turned to him. "You probably shouldn't play with my hair like that," she murmured, not quite looking at him.

"Why not?" he asked with a puzzled look. "I think it's beautiful. I think *you're* beautiful."

"Well, you just can't say things like that or do things like that!" she exclaimed, putting her hands on her hips. "It's just not fair."

"Why not? Why isn't it fair?" Josh responded, hoping he'd get her to say what she was really feeling. He put his own hands on his hips and waited.

She sputtered a bit, but finally said, "Because. Because you'll be going back to Texas in a couple of days. That's why."

Josh caught her to him and held her tight in his arms. "Oh, Jenny. That's what I'm trying to tell you, but I'm not doing a good job of it. I'm here for you, as long as you want me. I may be in Texas, but you can call on me anytime. *You're* why I asked to stay and help Zach with the ranchwork. I wanted to give us time to get to know each other."

She lifted her head from his chest and stared at him. Looking amazed, she whispered, "You stayed for me? Really?"

"Yes, for you."

Jenny threw her arms around his neck, rose on tiptoe, and hugged him. "Oh, Josh, I figured when you went back to Texas, I'd never see you again."

He hugged her back, and gave her a little kiss.

"Well, that's not going to happen, not if I have anything to say about it. You'll see me again."

The phone rang. It was Tillie reporting in as requested—home, safe and sound.

Josh said something about turning in.

Jenny countered with maybe he could stay just a little longer.

Sitting across from each other at the table didn't seem enough, so Josh sat in the old wooden rocker with Jenny cuddled on his lap. They talked and made plans for Sunday and the next few days. Josh wanted to visit Chris's grave before he left, and with a little gentle persuasion, he convinced Jenny to allow him to accompany her to the reading of the wills on Tuesday.

She was actually grateful for his offer. She had been dreading the legal proceedings, but they were necessary to clear Chip's guardianship and the ranch ownership.

Sunday dawned bright and beautiful. The blue skies seemed even larger, Josh noticed as he walked up to the house. Must be where that "Big Sky" name came from, he mused. He loved Texas, but this magnificient country could grow on a man.

He tapped on the back door, opened it and called Jenny's name.

"Come on in. We're almost ready."

Josh greeted her cheerfully with a smile and a quick kiss.

"Morning, Jen. You look awfully pretty this morning."

His caramel eyes skimmed warmly over her light blue dress. A string of bright blue beads around her neck picked up the bright blue of her eyes. She wore her hair gathered at the nape of her neck with a large, black barrette.

"Why, thank you, cowboy. You're looking pretty spiffy yourself," she countered with a grin. Josh wore his brown suit—the only one he'd brought with him—over a white shirt.

Jenny turned to Chip, wiped his face, and lifted him down from his high chair.

"Hey, Chip," Josh said to the smiling boy, "let's put your jacket on, and we'll take a ride to church."

Jenny drove "Baby" since Chip's carseat was already in place. When they got to Turk, she turned down a side street to a small white church.

This had been Jenny's church all her life. Some of her happiest memories originated here, and also some of her saddest. Her parents' funerals, and more recently, of course, the devastating double funeral for her brother and sister-in-law. As she sat down with Josh and Chip in a pew near the back, she took a moment to thank God for her friends and neighbors. Their support had been a great comfort to her these past weeks.

After the service ended, Jenny chatted with sev-

eral members of the congregation and introduced
Josh to them. Word had gotten around about the
Texan who had come to visit. In such a small
town, there had been speculative gossip which
was mostly pleasant, but ugly at times. In fact,
Bart Jones had freely spread rumors to whomever
would listen the past few days, while Tillie Ginn
had set a few minds straight in a hurry.

When Jenny, Josh and Chip left the church,
they walked up the hill that led to the cemetery.
More recent markers sat alongside weather-worn
stones of long ago. Jenny stopped at the Courter
plot.

The wind had picked up while they were inside
the church and the cedars, pine trees and tall lilac
bushes scattered among the gravesites were inad-
equate protection. The stiff breeze whipped
Jenny's skirt and hair. She tied Chip's hood se-
curely, as Josh held him.

"This is it," she murmured, and Josh barely
heard her over the wind. "I always stop by after
church for a minute or two."

Josh looked at the graves, their newness attest-
ing to the recent accident, then at Jenny. Her eyes
were closed, and there was a pinched look about
her face. He looked down at Chip who had stuck
his thumb in his mouth and snuggled against
Josh's shoulder.

A lump rising in his throat, he looked at the

unmarked graves. Solemnly and without reservation, he pledged to Chris and Sue his undying love and support for their little boy. He told Chris how much he loved Jenny, and how sorry he was that it had taken a tragedy to bring them together, but if she'd have him, he meant to marry her and be with her the rest of his life. He kissed the top of Chip's head and put his right arm around Jenny's slim shoulders. She turned to him and slipped an arm behind his back. They held each other for several quiet minutes.

Chapter Eight

The wind brought in storm clouds from the west that afternoon. The Courter Ranch was covered by eight inches of snow overnight. It was a typical spring storm that hits Montana at least once a year: a lot of heavy, wet snow, though not very cold. A beautiful snowstorm to the eye that can be deadly. The type of spring storm that snapped branches and power lines and caused ranchers to worry about new calves being born out in the pastures.

Zach and Josh rode out mid-morning to check on any newborns. Josh rode Chris's stallion, Vanguard, and Zach rode Bessie, the sorrel he'd owned for a few years. The sure-footed horses picked their way carefully through the sloppy

97

snow. The bright sun caused them to squint under the wide brims of their hats.

Most of the herd was in a pasture close to the barns, as they were used to being fed there. They stared curiously at the riders who paused to look them over. The men needed to check the farthest reaches of the ranch, where the cows tended to go when they were due to calve.

The riders separated and made a wide circle of the outlying areas. The ranch was fenced, but there were sheltered areas—stands of trees, hills, gullies and ravines—where a cow could hide.

Zach found a calf about six hours old. The mother bellowed in warning, but she allowed him to lift the calf across his saddle. The man mounted and coaxed the cow to follow them back to the barn.

Halfway there, Josh caught up with them. He had a newborn calf, barely an hour old, in his arms with its mother trailing behind.

Josh commented, "I didn't see any others." Zach agreed.

The men soon had the calves bedded down in dry straw after a rubdown with warm rags. The little ones now stood a much better chance of surviving.

Jenny had watched for them to come back to the barn, as she bundled Chip in boots and a parka. They followed the path that Josh had shoveled earlier.

Josh looked up and flashed them a warm smile when he heard them come through the door. Jenny lifted Chip to sit on the top of the partition, and Josh held him steady from the inside of the stall. Josh asked Jenny if it was okay for Chip to pet the calf.

"Sure. Do you want to pet the baby calf?" she asked the boy, who was already lifting his arms to Josh to get down.

Josh held his little hand and showed him how to stroke the calf's neck. Though excited, the boy patted gently.

He looked at Jenny and said, "Ba-by, Jen-jen, ba-by!" laughing delightedly. Josh and Jenny exchanged a smile over Chip's head and laughed themselves.

She thought, *What a wonderful man Josh is. He'd make a good father. What am I thinking? He's not going to propose marriage. Besides, with all that's happened, I can't consider taking on a husband. Anyway, why would Josh want a ready-made family? He should be having children of his own.* But why did the idea of Josh having babies with an other woman upset her?

Jenny prepared lunch, and after they'd eaten Josh moved Chip's carseat to the backseat of the Jeep.

The temperature had climbed steadily and now the snow was starting to melt. Josh knew the four-wheel-drive Jeep could easily get down the lane and out onto the main road. He and Jenny were going to shop for a new pickup in Bozeman.

Three hours later, they found one to Jenny's liking that had all the features Josh and Zach had discussed the night before. In fact, it was almost a duplicate of the truck that had been lost in the accident, only three years newer. Though Josh tried, he couldn't convince Jenny to let him buy a brand-new model—she insisted on a used truck. She was still a bit hesitant to accept Josh's offer, which was why she wanted a used vehicle. It would be easier to pay him back.

They had decided that Josh would drive the Jeep and she the truck back to the ranch. But Josh suggested they go shopping first as there was something he wanted to buy.

Jenny and Chip walked the length of the mall and back again and were seated on a bench when Josh joined them. Seeing nothing in his hands, Jenny gave him a questioning look.

"No luck finding what you wanted?" she asked.

"Oh, I found just the thing. I ran it out to the Jeep before I came to find you. The other package is tiny enough to fit in my jacket pocket," he added as he sat down on the bench.

Hmmmm, she thought, *tiny, huh. A little tiny*

something. She quickly tamped down the little burst of excitement that coursed through her veins. Probably for a girlfriend back home. She wanted to believe that he didn't have some beautiful girl back in Dallas, but what were the odds? He was too good-looking and nice, and obviously well-off, not to have marriage-minded females after him. The thought depressed her.

Josh pulled her back to the present with, "While we're here, is there anything you need, Jen?"

"Not really. Besides, I haven't much cash with me," she added, while watching Chip scramble up onto Josh's lap.

"That's no problem. This is my day to buy."

"Well, I do need disposable diapers, and they *would* be cheaper here."

"Okay. You lead the way." He stood and settled Chip on one hip, looking as if it were something he'd been doing for years. It brought a smile to Jenny's face.

Josh pushed the cart, and Chip rode in the seat while Jenny collected diapers and a few other baby items. She picked out ingredients for a salad to go with the hamburgers she planned to cook that night. As an afterthought, she grabbed a ten pound bag of potatoes. Zach liked french fries and, Josh probably did, too.

As Josh loaded the bags into the front of her new red and white truck, Jenny settled Chip into his carseat. When he came back from returning the cart, Jenny opened the door to the driver's side of the truck, but Josh stopped her with a hand on her arm.

Startled, she looked up into his dark eyes as he planted a firm kiss on her lips. When he raised his head, she touched a finger to her lips.

She exhaled and asked, "W—what was that for?"

"Been wanting to kiss you all day," was his answer. He gave her a boost up into the truck and closed her door.

Looking back at him through the window, she gave him a bright smile which he happily returned, then joined Chip in the Jeep for the drive home.

That evening after supper, the dishes washed and dried, Jenny and Josh bathed Chip.

"He's had a busy day," she stated as she wriggled him into his pajamas, despite his grumpy protests.

"J-ossh," Chip cried and demanded to be picked up. Josh sat in the rocker and held the boy against him. Chip snuggled into his broad shoulder and stuck his thumb into his mouth and, before long, dropped off to sleep.

After rocking him for awhile, Josh looked at Jenny and whispered, "Holding him feels so good,

I hate to put him down. He seems to have gotten used to me. I hope he doesn't give you a hard time after I go back to Texas."

"I know he'll miss you," she said, deliberately not looking at Josh's face as she lifted Chip from his arms and carried him across the room to his crib. She tried to hide the fact that she'd miss Josh, too.

Back downstairs, Josh sat in the middle of the living room floor and read the assembly directions for the Palomino horse he'd bought that day for Chip's birthday. It was the type that fit in a frame and was suspended on sturdy springs, so the rider could bounce and rock his pony without leaving one spot. Jenny found the screwdriver and crescent wrench Josh needed in a drawer on the back-porch, then kicked off her soft slippers and sat in a corner of the cream, blue and rose patterned sofa with her legs curled under her.

"Chip is going to love that. It's so nice of you to think of his birthday," she murmured as she watched him at work. She smiled at a couple of Josh's grunted words as he tightened the springs evenly on the horse.

"Well, I'll likely be gone when his actual day comes, so if you'll get this out and put a big, red bow on it, it can be from all of us, if you'd like."

"You're very thoughtful, Josh. Yes, I'll keep it in the back bedroom," she answered, referring to the room across from the office where her father had slept the last few years of his life. "I plan to get a new book or two for him, too. I was looking at them just last week. I can wrap them so he'll have a package to tear open."

"Yep, unwrapping is half the fun," he agreed with a grin.

Josh finished the job and stashed the horse where Jenny showed him. She put the tools away, and he gathered the paper and cardboard box to take out to a shed later. Zach had pointed out the bins they used to sort recyclable materials.

The coffee pot was empty, so Jenny offered Josh cola, beer or juice from the refrigerator. They then carried their drinks into the living room. Jenny went to the stereo and put in a CD of some of her favorite tunes, then joined Josh at the other end of the sofa.

"Nice," he commented on the music. "This is a comfortable room, Jenny, very pleasant. Tell me a little about the house. It must date back a ways."

She set her cola on the endtable nearest her, then answered, "Yes, but actually the first house on the place was the log cabin we use as the bunk-house now. When great-grandfather Courter married and began having children, he decided to build a larger house. So, over a few years time, he built this one. The story is that he'd picked this spot in the stand of trees for his permanent house when he first settled here."

She exchanged a smile with her listener, then continued, warming to her subject. She felt comfortable talking with Josh.

"There've been some changes over the years—bathrooms added, a furnace put in, Mom and Dad remodeled the kitchen a couple years before she died. Sue and Chris modernized the upstairs bathroom, and Sue worked long hours removing the old dark varnish on the woodwork in this room and the hall and re-papering the walls. She bought a few pieces of new furniture, too, like this sofa. She really brightened up this room, I think."

"Did it bother you to have her change your home?" Josh asked curiously.

"Oh, no," she replied as she tucked her legs under her. "It was her home, too. In fact, more so than mine. When I was about to go to college we assumed I'd leave home and work somewhere else, or maybe marry and move away someday. Besides, Chris and Sue owned the ranch by this time, though Dad had left me a third interest in it.

Chris saw that I had enough money for tuition, my car and anything else I needed. He was very fair."

"I can't imagine him being any other way," Josh agreed. "About the reading of the wills tomorrow," he noticed her frown and reached across the space between them to take her hand in his. "Are you worried about how it might affect your future with Chip? And whether you can keep the ranch?"

"Yes," she answered quietly, turning to face him. "I don't know exactly how it was set up. I'm just assuming I'll become Chip's guardian. It just makes me a little nervous—waiting to hear."

"Of course it does. I understand that. But it'll work out, and don't forget that I'm here for you." He lifted her left hand to his lips and gently kissed her fingers.

A little shiver skittered down her spine. *He actually kissed my hand!* She looked away from him, trying to hide her reaction. She just wasn't used to a man doing something like that. *Bet you could get used to it,* that little voice said.

Jenny sighed. "Thank you, Josh."

He sat back and seemed to be in deep thought for several minutes. Then he said, "Look, Jen, I've hesitated to ask you this, but I *do* have a business degree. If you'd let me, I'd like to look at the ranch operations account. I'm sure Chris has a cash flow chart. From what you've said, you're worried about immediate cash for operation over the summer. Would you look at it with me?" He gave her a coaxing smile, hoping she'd agree.

Though surprised at his offer, she quickly agreed.

"Let's do that. I should have thought of it before; I don't know where my mind has been."

"Now, we both know the answer to that. Caring for Chip and the house, mourning your loss, worrying about the future. You've done well, Jenny. A lot fell to you very suddenly, and I'm proud of how you're handling it all."

Jenny wanted to thank him again, but the words wouldn't come. She just nodded mutely as she looked at him, but her expressive eyes told him how she felt.

Josh moved closer and wrapped her in his strong arms. She sighed contentedly and laid her head on his chest. They sat together quietly for a time. He stroked her long soft hair, and she listened to the steady beat of his heart. *I could really get used to this,* she thought, then raised her head when Josh said her name.

Loosening his hold on her, he reached into his shirt pocket.

"I've got something for you. I hope you like it."

He pulled out a slender, green velvet box and handed it to her.

"Josh, you didn't need to buy me anything," she protested, but looked at him with shining eyes. "Oh, my, this is lovely," she murmured, as she opened the jewelry box.

It was an opal surrounded by tiny diamonds on

a gold chain. As Jenny lifted it from the case, the opal caught the lamplight and glowed among the sparkling diamonds.

"Thank you, Josh. It's beautiful. Was this the 'tiny little something' you bought today at the mall?" she asked with a sideways glance. She opened the clasp and handed it to him. Sweeping her thick hair up and to one side, she bared her neck to him.

Taking a deep breath to steady his unsteady hands, he managed to fasten the tiny clasp.

"I'm happy you like it. When I realized it was your birthstone, I wanted to get it for you. I hope you'll wear it tomorrow for good luck when we go to the lawyer's office."

Looking down at the pendant where it nestled against her sweater, she whispered, "I will. I'll always treasure it, Josh. Thank you so much."

Lifting her arms around his neck, she did something she hadn't done before. She kissed him first, and a sweet kiss it was.

Kissing Jenny was just plain wonderful. There was something different about her—a sweet, lovely innocence—that seemed to wrap around his lonely heart. This was definitely the girl he'd been hoping to find.

"Let's look at the ranch records, honey," he urged and followed her to the office.

Turning on a lamp, Jenny sat at the desk and

turned on the computer. Pulling up the cash flow chart, which covered the past year and the near future, she gave the chair to Josh. She dragged a smaller chair over and sat beside him to view the screen.

Josh was quiet while he scrolled through the past twelve months. He then backtracked to point out some major items.

"I'm surprised that Chris has a loan to pay off, Jen. Of course, it's been a few years since his rodeo days, but he won big money for several years."

"Well, I was just a kid then, so I don't think anyone ever told me what he'd won. But when Dad got sick, there were a lot of bills to pay. Dad had no health insurance, and I suspect that's where a lot of his money went. That, and investing back into the ranch each year."

"Yeah, that makes sense. Every rancher has good and bad years, what with cattle prices fluctuating, and the weather," Josh speculated.

"It looks like he was making quarterly installments on that loan, and the next payment is due June 1st." Josh made a mental note of the amount due. "Is there information on checking and savings accounts?" he asked.

"Yes, there they are," she replied as the menu came up on the screen.

They checked the balances and saw that while

the checking account was low, there was more than enough in savings to cover the next loan payment.

Jenny said, "Sue had a small checking account that she used for household things—groceries and such. And I have my own, too—though it is getting low," she admitted with a sigh.

"Don't worry, Jen. Tomorrow will settle things, and you can put your name on all the accounts at the bank and pay any upcoming bills."

"There will be life insurance, but I want to put most of that away for Chip's future. I want to have a nice marker made for their graves, too."

Josh turned off the computer. Sliding his chair back, he turned toward her. "Jenny, everyone should have a little sister as kind and loving as you." He kissed her briefly on her forehead.

She looked surprised, then a frown appeared. *He's looking at me as a little sister, again. Our kisses obviously don't mean as much to him as they do to me. But I guess I shouldn't be surprised.* She tried not to think of all the other women—much more glamorous and experienced women than she—that he'd kissed. *I probably rank at about the bottom of the list,* she thought miserably. She got up quickly and returned the chair to its usual spot.

Chapter Nine

"Is something wrong?" Josh asked, standing as she did.

"Oh, no. I guess I'm just worried about tomorrow." She turned off the lamp and followed him to the hall. "Thanks for looking over the accounts with me. I—I'm tired. I'd like to try to get a good night's sleep."

"Sure, Jen. I should get down to the bunkhouse anyway, before Zach sends out a search party." He grinned at her sober countenance, trying to bring a smile.

It worked, briefly.

"Goodnight, Josh."

" 'Night, Jenny. What time should I come up in the morning?"

"Leaving at nine-thirty should give us enough time," she replied. Josh bid her good night and left her there in the hall.

He locked the back door behind him. As he walked down the path to the bunkhouse, he worried about what had cooled her attitude just a few minutes ago. Maybe he was reading her wrong, and she didn't like him as much as he thought. He paused outside the door, and looked up at the full moon in the clear night sky, and made a wish on the man in the moon. Something he hadn't done since he was a young boy in Texas.

The next morning, Josh insisted on driving the Jeep. As they were running late, and Chip's car-seat was still in it, she agreed and they were soon on their way.

Though Jenny looked a bit tired, she talked pleasantly enough about the countryside they were passing through.

"Just a little way ahead now, we'll go down a hill into what's called Alder Gulch. That's where a huge gold strike was made in 1863, and it's what brought many people to the area, including my great-grandpa."

"That's interesting," Josh commented. "During the War between the States?"

"That's right, only we call it the Civil War up here, Texan," she corrected kiddingly.

Josh laughed and felt relieved that they seemed to be on an even keel again.

"At the height of the gold rush, it was quite a boom town, and for a decade or so was the territorial capital. Now, it's still the county seat, even though only about a hundred and fifty people are year-round residents. But it's a busy tourist attraction in the summer."

"Why's that? Because of the gold strike all those years ago?" Josh asked, looking briefly at her.

Jenny made a pretty picture in a deep red pantsuit worn over a black turtleneck sweater. It pleased him to see his gift hanging around her neck.

"Yes, that's commemorated, as well as other interesting events, like the vigilantes that took the law into their own hands when miners were being robbed and killed. But the big attractions are the preserved historical buildings. Of course, there's Boot Hill Cemetery, guided tours, daily entertainment. I could go on and on!" she finished with a laugh.

"I like hearing you," Josh said, "and it sounds real interesting. I'd like to see it all one day."

"Well, it's mostly closed this early in the year, but it'll be in full swing in the summer months."

"I'll plan on coming back then."

Jenny looked over at him quickly, then away.

That's the second time he's made a comment about doing something here later. Will he really come back?

They reached the town and Jenny showed him where to park near the stately old courthouse building. Josh admired the style and stonework of the structure as they climbed the steps from the street and walked up to its doors.

They found the lawyer's office and sat in the outer room only briefly before being shown in. Just enough time to help Chip out of his jacket and for Jenny to take a deep, calming breath.

Ned Newhouse greeted them cordially. Jenny introduced the silver-haired gentleman to Josh, then sat down with Chip on her lap. Josh sat beside her in a matching chair.

The lawyer offered coffee, but both declined. Jenny cuddled Chip close, seeking comfort in his presence, while she waited for Mr. Newhouse to go on.

"All right then, let's begin. Since I was told that Mrs. Courter predeceased her husband," words that made Jenny flinch, "I'll read her last will and testament first." He cleared his throat and adjusted his wire-rimmed glasses.

Sue's will was short. They learned that she had left anything she owned to her husband for his lifetime, then to her son.

Chris's was much longer and more detailed. His

two-thirds interest in the Courter Ranch was left to his wife for her lifetime, then it would be passed down to his son.

If Sue remarried, then his interest would go to his son, with Sue as administrator, until Chip's twenty-first birthday.

If his wife predeceased him, his share of the ranch would go directly to his son with the proviso that his sister, Jennifer Lea Courter, would act as administrator of the ranch until his son reached his twenty-first birthday.

In the circumstance of his son being orphaned before attaining his majority, guardianship would pass to his sister.

Jenny breathed a sigh of relief and loosened her grip on Chip, unaware that she had been holding him so tightly. The boy had been unusually quiet on her lap, as if he had been listening, too.

She looked over at Josh and caught his warm smile.

Mr. Newhouse concluded the reading and cleared his throat again.

"As you can see, it is set up in a way that most young married couples with children would choose, assuring the continuity of the ranch holdings and the security of their son. I'm sure that over the years, if they had lived, they would have occasionally updated the will. Are there any questions, Miss Courter?" he asked kindly, as he re-moved his glasses.

"No, I don't believe so. It reassures me to hear that Chris wanted me to be Chip's guardian. I don't know what I would've done if I had to give him up." Tears of relief blurred her vision, and she dug in her purse for a tissue, but Josh was quick with his clean white handkerchief. "Thank you," she murmured his way.

"Sir," Josh began, "I have a few questions. Jenny has bills to pay soon. Will her brother's life insurance and truck insurance be released to her, now that she's Chip's legal guardian? I hate to bring it up, but what inheritance taxes will have to be paid? Then there's the question of Jenny being able to use the ranch accounts at the bank."

"All good questions, young man. Yes, the wills will be filed today and a copy sent to you," nodding in Jenny's direction. "As executor, I'll rush a request for release of all insurance funds. You should go to the bank tomorrow to change the signature cards for the accounts. As for the tax bill, look for it in the mail within the month. But since you already own a third of the ranch prop-erty, it will be reduced accordingly."

Josh nodded, and Jenny expressed her thanks to the lawyer.

He came around the desk to shake her hand.

"I am sorry for your loss, Miss Courter. If

there's ever any way I can be of service, just give me a call. And, if I may add, I can see that this youngster will be in very good hands."

"Thank you, Mr. Newhouse," replied Jenny, rewarding the older man with a brilliant smile.

"And my thanks, as well, sir," Josh added.

Back outside on the street the sun was shining brightly and the temperature had risen several degrees. Jenny looked around and lifted her arms to the Big Sky.

"Isn't it simply a glorious day!" she exclaimed, her voice full of the joy and happiness she felt.

"It sure is," Josh agreed. He lifted Chip high and swung him around, and the boy dissolved in giggles. Josh settled him back on his left hip and put his right arm around Jenny. "It's so good to know that Chip will be able to stay with you. Let's celebrate! I know it's not the tourist season yet, but we can surely find something to do."

"You bet!" Jenny agreed enthusiastically.

They strolled along the old-fashioned wooden sidewalks of Virginia City. Though the stores were closed for another month or so, Josh enjoyed reading the signs and looking around. He was particularly interested in the home of the first territorial newspaper, and the opera house, where daily melodramas were enacted.

"We've got to come back here in-season, Jen. I'd love to get a better look at it all."

Jenny appreciated his thought.

"That'd be fun, Josh," she replied, slipping her hand into his.

They decided to look for an eatery that was open year round and soon found one on a side street. They enjoyed a pleasant lunch in comfortable surroundings decorated in a nineteenth century motif.

Jenny chose a toasted cheese sandwich for Chip, along with French fries.

"I'll have to be sure he gets some green vegetables at supper," she commented, with a smile for the happy boy. He enjoyed smearing catsup around on his plate—and elsewhere.

"This is good," he said, indicating his stew with his fork, "but not as good as your stew, Jen."

Jenny's face flushed with happiness. She was not used to compliments on her culinary skills.

"Why, thank you." She sipped from her water glass, and went on. "I'm not really very good at many things. Mom died young, and she hadn't gotten around to teaching me much. I sort of taught myself after that, but Dad and Chris were easy to please—meat and potatoes men. Dad especially liked fried potatoes, so if I cooked them every night, he was happy. At least no one starved," she concluded with a chuckle.

Josh chuckled, too, and said, "Well, I guess I'm a meat and potatoes man myself. Oh, I eat in fancy restaurants sometimes at some of the business dinners I have to attend, but what I enjoy most is spending days on the ranch and filling up on Consuela's wonderful Tex-Mex food."

"I remember you mentioning her. She's your housekeeper and the ranch foreman's wife?"

"Yep. Gabe Martinez. You'd like them both, I'm sure. Old Gabe means as much to me as I think Zach means to you."

"That's a lot then," she answered. "Say, Tillie and Zach seemed to have had a good time babysitting last Saturday. Did he say anything about it to you?"

Josh grinned across the table. "He did, as a matter of fact. Tillie invited him to supper tonight. He asked if you or I would be using the new pickup, and I said I didn't think so."

Jenny's eyes lit up, and she exclaimed, "Wonderful! Wouldn't it be grand if they got together after all these years? They're two of my favorite people in the whole world."

"Well, let's not count our chickens," he joked. "But, I'm all for people being happy." *Including you and me,* he thought, as he watched her clean off Chip's fingers. *She's going to be a super mother to that boy. Chip, old fellow, you are so lucky to have her love.*

* * *

Over the next few days, Jenny was so relieved to have Chip's guardianship settled, she went about the house doing her chores with a smile on her face, humming happy tunes. It may have been her imagination, but Chip seemed happier, too. That realization made her feel guilty. Perhaps he was feeding off her emotions, which meant her earlier worry hadn't been good for the little fellow.

Josh and Zach were also in high spirits, and since Josh planned to return to Dallas on Saturday, they busied themselves with some barn repairs. He learned from Zach that Chris had intended to paint the barn that spring, so Josh made arrangements for a painting crew to come out the following week to paint the large barn and the smaller outbuildings white. He planned to talk Jenny into letting him pay for the job, maybe as a gift in Chris's memory. That might work, but by now he knew how stubborn she could be.

On Wednesday Jenny made a trip to town to take care of the signature cards at the bank. Josh came up to the house to watch Chip while she was away.

The following day, she took Chip to Beth's "Pooh Bear Daycare" for an hour of playtime, and picked up the mail while she visited with Tillie. Her friend was pleased to know that things seemed to be settled, and when asked, told Jenny how much she had enjoyed cooking a meal for Zach last Tuesday. Jenny was surprised but tickled to see a slight blush color her cheeks.

"Hmm, are you and Zach getting to be an item, Tillie?" she teased gently.

"My goodness, girl. Don't be silly. We're much too old for that kind of foolishness," Tillie said, but Jenny noticed the twinkle in her eyes.

Later, back at the ranch, Jenny prepared a lunch for her two favorite hardworking cowboys. The men went back to work; she tidied the kitchen and put Chip down for his nap.

She decided to bake a cake, but before beginning she took a critical look at the kitchen and back porch floors. The sloppy snow earlier in the week and the subsequent mud had left tracks on the linoleum.

Now's a good chance to mop, while Chip's asleep, she thought to herself. She pulled a mop bucket, cleanser, and a sponge mop from the laundry room off the kitchen. In short order, she was scrubbing away when she heard a knock at the front door.

Jenny was startled as she hadn't heard a vehicle approach. She propped the mop, dried her damp hands on her jeans, and went to the window. She was surprised to see that it was not Bart's truck. It was an unfamiliar white Honda. Jenny's brow creased in a frown, and she left the chain on the door when she opened it a few inches.

"Yes?" she asked.

The unsmiling middle-aged woman was dressed in a neat navy suit, and carried a navy purse and a brown leather briefcase. Slung over her left arm was a teal raincoat.

"Miss Jennifer Courter?"

"That's right," Jenny replied.

"My name is Priscilla Hamilton. I'm from the county welfare office." As she spoke, she showed Jenny her credentials, then returned them to her purse. "I'd like to talk with you, please, about your nephew."

For a moment Jenny thought her heart had stopped. It started again with an almost painful pang. Moving the security chain with trembling fingers, she managed to open the door for Ms. Hamilton. *Oh no, please don't let anything go wrong now.*

"Of course," she heard herself say in as normal a voice as she could muster. "Come in."

The woman entered the front hall, then the living room when Jenny indicated it. Walking behind her, Jenny glanced at her reflection in a wall mirror and frantically tried to tuck the loose strands of hair back into the braid she wore. She looked in dismay at her stockinged feet. Too late to do anything about them now.

"Is there a problem?" Jenny asked as she sat in a chair opposite the couch where Miss Hamilton—somehow Jenny knew she was a 'miss'—sat primly on the edge. Placing her briefcase on the coffee table, she extracted some forms. "When my nephew's parents died, a lady named Mrs. Gilbert came out and seemed satisfied that Chip would be fine with me."

"Yes, I have her report right here. Mrs. Gilbert has retired this past month."

Jenny felt her spirits drop. *Shoot, Mrs. Gilbert had been wonderfully kind and supportive—a grandmotherly type.* She wasn't sure she liked her replacement.

Continuing, Miss Hamilton said, "We've received notification from Probate Court of the wills being filed, and while we do try to honor a parent's selection of guardianship, in this case, some questions have been raised."

"Oh really, what kind of questions?"

Jenny decided she *definitely* didn't like this woman. She felt as if she was being examined for defects and not passing inspection. That brought Jenny's temper up, though she reminded herself not to let it show—at least not yet.

"First, you're a very young woman. Are you sure you feel able to take on the responsibility of an infant? I feel duty-bound to remind you that it is a commitment of many years' duration—you can't just change your mind next month or next year," the social worker warned.

Jenny sucked in an indignant breath before she replied.

"Ms. Hamilton, it is true that I'm young. I was twenty-one last October as you probably already know. But many women my age have children and raise them satisfactorily. I love Chip. I'm his only living blood relative, and I'll do whatever is necessary to give him a good home."

Hoping that her words came across as sincerely as she meant them, Jenny was startled—astounded was a better word—at Miss Hamilton's next sentence.

"All well and good, Miss Courter, but our office received a complaint yesterday from a Mr. Bart Jones. He says that the moral welfare of your nephew is being endangered by the presence of a male visitor in your home. Is there a man living here with you?"

Jenny felt her mouth drop open. Then her temper surfaced. *What is that Bart Jones trying to do?* She sat forward, her face pale, and spoke from her heart.

"Yes, I do have a visitor, Ms. Hamilton, and Bart Jones knows that. He also knows that Mr. Brady was a good friend of my brother's. When he heard of Chris's death, he came up to pay his respects and check on me and his friend's child.

He's a courteous and honorable man who has shown me only respect. Chip enjoys his company, too. My foreman, Zach Knutson, and he have become friends. Josh has stayed on for a few days to give him a hand about here and to lend me moral support," she answered, angry with herself for allowing her voice to quiver.

"But you haven't fully answered the question, Miss Courter. Is the man living with you?"

Jenny leaped to her feet, her hands clenched at her sides. "No, he is not. But why take my word for it. Look around the house. I'm sure you need to do that while you're here anyway. Am I correct?"

"Well, yes," the woman replied and got to her feet to follow Jenny, as she was already leading the way out of the room.

"This is the kitchen. Please watch your step as I was mopping the floor when you arrived. Back porch, a downstairs bathroom," Jenny briskly pushed open the door to allow Miss Hamilton to look in.

"Down this hall is the ranch office," she said, as she again opened a door. "Opposite is an unused bedroom," she pointed out, knowing that Miss Hamilton could see no evidence of anyone using it.

"Now please follow me upstairs, but I must ask you to move quietly. Chip is taking his nap."

Miss Hamilton looked a bit disconcerted, and Jenny began to enjoy herself. *Just let her try to see any sign of Josh sleeping here,* she thought, with a toss of her pretty head.

Chapter Ten

Upstairs, she turned to her right and showed the woman her bedroom. Jenny wordlessly opened her drawers and closet to demonstrate the absence of any male belongings.

"This room across the hall has been used for storage lately." Stepping inside, Miss Hamilton looked around briefly. A bed devoid of bedding, an empty dresser, some boxes and trunks, and a dressmaker's dummy greeted her. Not saying a word, she returned to the hall.

"The master bedroom. All of Chris and Sue's things are still here. I haven't had the heart to go through them yet," Jenny added with a sigh. "Across the hall is Chip's room." They slipped into the cheerfully decorated room long enough for the social worker to see that it contained all the things a baby needed. She stood by the crib looking down at the sleeping baby for several moments, before the two women returned to the living room.

"Thank you for the tour, and I do get your point. Mr. Brady is obviously not living in this house. And both the house and child look well cared for." Miss Hamilton tendered a smile toward Jenny, who felt a lessening of tension. "But, I *am* curious. Where *does* Mr. Brady sleep?"

"Why, down in the bunkhouse, ma'am," came a Texas drawl from the doorway to the kitchen.

Startled, both women turned toward his voice. Miss Hamilton's mouth decidedly gaped, but Jenny gave Josh a welcoming smile. Indeed, she was glad to have his back-up in this unexpected meeting with the social worker.

"Excuse me, ladies, but I called your name from the back porch, Jenny, and you didn't hear me."

"I was giving Ms. Hamilton a tour of the house, Josh. Priscilla Hamilton, this is Joshua Brady, the man in question." Jenny made the introduction with a flourish. "Ms. Hamilton was sent out by the welfare office to check up on me and Chip."

"Oh? Why is that necessary, ma'am?" he asked politely, as his face grew sober.

"Let's sit down," Jenny intervened, but Josh

said his jeans were too dirty for the living room, and so they adjourned to the kitchen. Jenny suggested coffee, and in a minute or two, they were seated around the table with steaming mugs in hand.

"What brought you up to the house, Josh?" Jenny inquired.

He sat the mug on the table before he said, "Zach came in from the pasture and told me there was a strange car parked up here, so I thought I'd see if things were okay. Are they?"

Jenny shrugged and replied, "I'm not really sure. You see, Bart Jones is making trouble for me again."

"Please, fill me in." He looked from Jenny to Miss Hamilton questioningly.

"Well, Mr. Brady," the lady began rather stiffly, after carefully placing her mug on the blue placement before her. "The office received a complaint regarding the living situation here. We are required, of course, to look into all such complaints, so I came by this afternoon. Mr. Bart Jones is the source. Miss Courter assures me that no immoral behavior has occurred."

"That's correct, ma'am. As I said when I came in, I sleep in the bunkhouse. I'm sharing it with Zach Knutson, Jenny's foreman, while I'm visiting from Texas."

Jenny gave the social worker an *I told you so*

look. She glanced down at her hands then, and felt fortunate that the lady hadn't noticed the look.

"Yes, thank you, Mr. Brady, and it was evident when Miss Courter showed me around that such is the case. But why would this Mr. Jones start such a rumour?"

"That's easy to explain, ma'am. Bart has been harrassing Jenny for several weeks now. He and I sort of locked horns one day, and this is probably his way of getting even," Josh suggested as he pushed his cup aside and leaned forward earnestly to make his point, crossing his forearms on the table.

Jenny took up the story, "He got it into his head that he and I should get married. Well, I definitely don't want to marry him, for several reasons. One is that he's a lot older than I am, and another is that I just don't like the man. But he *is* our neighbor, so I tried to be polite. Since my brother and sister-in-law were killed, he's been coming over most days, and just won't leave when I ask him to." Jenny took a deep breath and tried not to get angry. "And Josh was helpful one day when I came home from town with groceries. Bart was waiting for me. Josh strongly suggested that Bart leave—verbally suggested, not physically,—and Bart was very angry."

Miss Hamilton sat back in her chair, a look of growing understanding on her face. "That explains it, then. I'll relay that to my supervisor, and I'm sure she'll write a strongly-worded letter to Mr. Jones. You may even want to have a restraining order issued."

"Not a bad idea, Jenny," Josh added. "I'd worry less about you and Chip after I leave on Saturday." He gave her a smile that melted away any anger she'd been feeling over the situation.

"I—I'll think about it." Then she sat bolt upright, and exclaimed, "Oh, that rat! This is what he meant."

"What?" Josh asked quickly, his eyes darkening with concern.

Even Miss Hamilton leaned forward, eagerly waiting for Jenny to continue.

"A week ago, I stopped for coffee at the Cowboy Cafe while Chip was at daycare playing with the other children for an hour or so. Bart came in and sat in my booth, even though I made it plain I didn't want him there. I told him I had nothing to say to him, but he implied that you and I, Josh, were carrying on, out here at the ranch. Only, he didn't use such polite words."

Josh bristled, and Jenny agitatedly twisted her napkin as she talked.

"Well, as you might guess," she looked at Josh, "I got mad and told him off. Some of the other people in the cafe heard me, and George—that's the owner—came over to the booth. He sort of gave Bart a look that said leave now or else."

"Good," Josh put in. "I'm glad someone took your side."

"Me, too," Jenny agreed. "But before he left, Bart told me I'd be sorry."

"Well," Miss Hamilton said in a huff, "he certainly has tried to upset things for you. But don't worry, I plan to explain it all to my supervisor, and to give you the best of recommendations. We had planned to honor your brother's request, despite your young age, Miss Courter, but we can't ignore such a rumor. We must always consider the well-being of the child involved."

She paused to drain her mug, as Jenny and Josh exchanged a happy and much relieved glance.

"I'll be going now. I appreciate your time, both of you. And, may I add, I personally think that little boy is very lucky to have an aunt like you, Jenny Courter."

With those words, she rose from the table. Jenny and Josh walked with her to the living room where she gathered her things, accepted Jenny's heartfelt thanks, and left.

Jenny closed the door behind her and turned to Josh. With a whoop, he swung her off her feet and around in a big circle. When he set her back down, he kept her in his arms. Jenny, who couldn't resist putting her arms around his neck, pulled him down for a kiss of pure joy.

Her words came out on a rush of air as she said, "Josh, I want to thank you for your help. For giving me your support in front of Ms. Hamilton." She looked up into his face, as she spoke. "Her unexpected visit unsettled me at first."

She's so beautiful, he thought, *and I want to tell her I love her, but it's probably much too soon. . . . Better keep it light, old man.*

"Honey, I was glad to help, but as far as I could see, you were doing fine. I'm happy we're off the hook with Ms. Hamilton," he said with a gentle smile.

"Me, too," she agreed, "but I was a little scared for a bit. Then I rather enjoyed giving her the grand tour, so she could see for herself that you weren't living in the house."

She gave him one last hug, which Josh returned warmly, then she stepped away from him.

Chip chose that moment to awake from his nap with a loud yell for Jenny. She looked at Josh in amazement.

"He called for *me*. He said Jen-jen," she cried, her face glowing.

"Let's go get him up, honey," Josh urged as he tugged on her hand.

Jenny hesitated. "But—but I don't want him to forget Sue," she whispered.

"It's okay, Jen. It's good that he's getting used to you being here for him."

"Yes," she agreed as she moved toward the stairs, "he's adjusting like my child psychology textbooks say he should. You're right, he'll be okay."

"Of course, I'm right."

"Don't be so smug, cowboy," she teased, as she ran ahead of him up the stairs.

The next twenty-four hours sped by much too quickly for Jenny. She knew that Josh had to go back to Texas, he had a business to attend to, after all. But she had so enjoyed his company and his input—not just monetary, but his ideas and thoughts. She did her best not to show her dread. She had gotten along before he arrived on her doorstep; she and Chip would manage just fine after he left. She had to remind herself at least once an hour that last day.

Jenny started the day by asking the men up to the house for a big breakfast of flapjacks and bacon. She had decided to make it a special day in every way that she could manage. When the men, including Chip, declared that they couldn't eat another bite, she stopped cooking and sat to eat her own short stack of cakes. The men drank another cup of coffee to keep her company while Chip polished off his milk. Jenny hadn't enjoyed a morning meal so much in a long time.

The day had warmed nicely by mid-morning. Jenny and Chip walked down to the barns to see what the cowpokes were up to, and found them taking it easy in the bunkhouse.

"We came to see what you two were doing, and it looks like we caught you loafing." Her laugh made it plain that she wasn't the least bit concerned.

"Yep," Zach agreed, "we're so filled up on your good cookin', we needed to just sit a spell before we could think about any more work."

"The other critters are fed, too, so we're all loafing," Josh added. "Say, Jen, Zach and I were wondering, if you could have the house painted, what color would you choose?"

Surprised, Jenny looked from one to the other, then sat down with them at the well-worn wooden table, where she had played innumerable checker games. Chip chose to clamber onto Zach's lap, where the man settled him comfortably.

A little smile on her face, she said, "Well, it's always been white, but it's been so long since it's been painted, the white hardly shows anymore. Sue and I talked about it once. We pictured it yellow with dark green doors and shutters. Thought that would be pretty against the grove of pines." Again, she looked at each of the men.

"Why? Are you two thinking of painting? I'm not sure if there's money for it."

"Zach's having a crew out next week to spray-paint the barns," Josh said casually, "since Chris had planned on doing that this spring. Now, don't fret about the cost, Jen," he said quickly, noticing her mouth about to open, "I plan to cover it as a gift to you all. Especially to Chris, as a sort of follow-through from me on what he'd planned. Okay, Jen?"

"I—I," she lowered her head and worried her lower lip. "I guess I should just accept graciously, shouldn't I? That's the polite thing to do, instead of arguing about it," she answered, as she looked at him from under her thick, black lashes. "Yes, Josh, I appreciate it very much, as you seem to really want to do it."

He grabbed her hand on the table and gave it a quick squeeze, grinning at her happily.

"Thanks, Jenny, I *really* do want to do it. Now, when the crew comes out next week, you have them give you an estimate on the house, so that can be taken care of soon. I like the idea of yellow. Sounds welcoming," Josh declared.

"Yep, right pretty," Zach added.

Jenny smiled, and said, "Here I am getting the whole place painted, and I actually came down to see if either of you had any laundry to add to the load up at the house."

"Oh, not really," Josh said, "I don't mind packing some dirty duds back to Dallas."

"Me neither, Jen. Besides, since this is Josh's last day here, I thought maybe you and he should have some fun. I called Tillie a bit ago, and she and I are offering to sit with this big fellow tonight," he said, as he jiggled Chip on his knees to the boy's delighted giggles. "Give you a chance to go out somewhere."

"Why, thanks Zach, that's really nice of you and Tillie. Want to, Jenny?" Josh asked.

"Sure, that'll be fun. Thanks, Zach," she added, with a pat on his denim-covered arm.

"I'll call Tillie back to let her know it's a go," he said, with a little twinkle in his eyes.

Jenny glanced at Josh and grinned, and he winked back. They were both thinking of Zach and Tillie growing closer, and it pleased them.

"Say, Jen, if you'll give me a chance to wash up a bit, I'd like to take you and Chip into town, maybe have lunch at that Cowboy Cafe you told me about."

"Okay. It's such a pretty day, I won't argue about anything," she laughed.

Josh, grinning devilishly, commented, "Now, you might regret saying that, honey."

Zach guffawed, and Jenny laughed, too. She swatted Josh's arm and got up from the table.

"Come on, Chip, this conversation is getting too

deep. See you up at the house, Josh. See you later, Zach."

Chip scrambled down. She took his hand, then leaned to plant a kiss on the old man's cheek. Turning, she caught Josh's eyes on her, and she wrinkled her nose at him before she and Chip strolled out the door.

She heard Josh and Zach laughing, and her heart felt so warm and happy she thought it could burst.

Jenny gathered Chip's things and put him into a clean pullover and, since the temperature had risen into the high fifties, added only a light-weight blue windbreaker with a hood just in case.

She looked very nice herself, a fact not unnoticed by Josh. She wore jeans, a cotton blouse in a beige and blue flowered print, and her comfortable black boots. Her hair hung long and free, the way Josh liked it.

Josh was wearing the shirt he'd borrowed from Chris's closet the day he'd bathed Chip. She'd never tell him how much she had enjoyed washing and ironing it for him. *A girl needed to keep a few secrets,* she thought as she glanced over at him.

"Say, it's a little early for lunch. Is there anywhere else you'd like to go before we stop at the Cowboy?" Jenny asked.

He grinned back at her, and replied, "I was just thinking that Turk is a small town, but I haven't seen much of it. Drive me around, and point out all the places of interest."

"Glad to oblige, sir," she returned, cheekily. "But, yes, it really is a small town—not too exciting."

Her heart thumped a bit harder when he said, "But *you* grew up here, so it's interesting to me."

Chip chose that moment to yell at a couple of cows in a field. "Moo-oo cows! Moo-oo cows!" he hollered happily, which brought a burst of laughter from Josh. Josh joined him in a chorus of cow calling for a minute or so which had Jenny laughing, too.

"Well, Mr. Brady," she intoned in her best tour guide voice, "we are now reaching the outskirts of the metropolis of Turk, Montana, population 750 on a good day. I'll show you places that have meant a lot to me over the years."

Turning right, she slowed and indicated a white, two-story frame house on her left. "That's where my best friend, Connie, lives, though she's at Bozeman going to college now. I shared an apartment with her and two other girls when I stayed during the week."

"I also spent a lot of time at her house, for sleep-overs and such. Her mom was always real nice to me; I expect she felt sorry for me after

Mom died. But, she didn't fuss over me too much. That wouldn't have been good."

"I'm glad you had your friend's mother, Jen," Josh said quietly and gently squeezed her shoulder.

"Me, too," she smiled and gulped at the tender look of caring in his caramel eyes. *Oh, my,* she thought, and quickly looked back at the road.

She swallowed, then went on. "Of course, you've seen the church," she said as she made a left, "but it's always been important to me, too. Sunday School, singing in the choir, Youth Group as a teen. People were so supportive of Chris and me when our folks died."

She paused, and Josh knew she was thinking the same thought about when Chris and Sue died.

"People in small towns tend to pull together, don't they? I think the same about Banjo," Josh inserted.

"Mm-hmm," she agreed.

After crossing a few more streets, she slowed and turned right.

"See that huge house ahead where the street ends? It's been fixed up and turned into a nursing home. When I was young, it was pretty run-down. Only two old women, lived in it, and we kids thought they were witches, especially at Halloween," she finished with a giggle. "We were so silly!"

Josh laughed and agreed with her judgement.

"Now, just one block over," she said, as she turned in the cul-de-sac before the nursing home, "is the hospital. Not big, by any means, but it's a comfort to have it so close for emergencies."

Josh agreed as they drove by. It was a modern L-shaped glass and stucco building.

Back on the main street, she waited for a truck to go by before crossing to the west side of town.

"Here is where I spent the major part of twelve years of my life," she kidded, and slowed the car even more as they neared the combination elementary, middle, and high school. Two sections were older with a much newer addition built between. To the back stretched a modern gymnasium. It all sat on several pleasant acres of grass and trees, with playground equipment, a track and baseball field. When she turned down a side street, Josh was interested to see wooden bleachers and a football field.

"I'm surprised. Is Turk big enough to field a football team?" he asked in amazement.

"Oh, football's very big in Montana. But, yes, they do field an eight-man team. There are several others in Madison and neighboring countries, enough to make up a league. A lot of little towns kept alive by the ranches and farms, timber and mining interests."

"And not all seeing eye to eye on what's important, right?" he asked thoughtfully.

"Right. It's a struggle, to be sure."

Neither said anything for a bit, until Jenny pointed out "Pooh Bear Daycare."

Chip squealed, "Bef!" when he spotted it.

Josh grinned, "That must be the daycare you take him to sometimes. He's pretty observant for a little fellow."

"Yes, Beth Grayson runs it. She's a great gal and a good friend, too. When I decided to major in elementary ed, I worked with her for several summers. The money came in handy for college, and the experience was valuable."

Chip said, "Bef," a few more times, and Jenny assured him he'd see Beth another day.

"Well, that's about all the grand tour I can muster up for you, sir, seeing as how you've been down the main drag before."

"Well, thank you then, ma'am, I appreciate the tour and your lovely company. I may even give you a tip, later on," he drawled, with a teasing grin her way.

"Uh-oh," she teased back, raising her eyebrows in mock alarm, and pulled into a diagonal parking slot near the Cowboy Cafe.

Chapter Eleven

Once inside the small restaurant, Josh hung his hat on a rack near the door, then picked up the toddler seat Jenny had asked him to bring to their table. Placing it on the chair next to Jenny, he lifted Chip onto it and secured the safety strap. Chip liked being up so close to the table.

"You're a big boy today, aren't you, Chip?" he said to the boy, who returned his smile.

"Yep, big!" he replied heartily, while spreading his little arms as wide as he could.

Jenny and Josh exchanged a look of amusement, and picked up the menus.

"Zach recommended the chicken-fried steak. What do you think?" Josh asked.

"It's very good. Hazel feeds that to a lot of hungry cowboys around here. She's quite a cook."

Josh looked across the cafe toward the man behind the cash register, who had just rung up a diner's tab.

"Is that the owner, Jen?" he asked, nodding in George's direction.

"Yes, that's George Bos. He and his wife, Hazel, run the place."

Looking thoughtful, Josh murmured, "Excuse me a minute, Jen. He's one of the reasons I wanted to come here."

Josh rose and crossed to the counter in a few long strides. He introduced himself, and, somehow, wasn't surprised that the man already knew who he was. He thanked George for the help he'd given Jenny earlier when Bart Jones had bothered her.

"You bet, son. Jenny's a special gal. My wife and I have known her all her life, and they don't make 'em any better. I was glad to give her a hand when Jones hassled her." He continued with a chuckle. "Though she was doing a good job of telling him off on her own."

"Well, thanks again. She is pretty special, isn't she?" Josh agreed with a smile.

George gave him a contemplative look, then asked directly, "You planning on staying around Turk, Josh?"

"Well, I'm heading back to Dallas tomorrow. I've got to tend to business down there," he answered, then glanced at Jenny and Chip across the room, "but I'm hoping to come back real soon."

George nodded understandingly, and said encouragingly, "You do that, son."

Josh grinned his thanks.

"Say, are you and Jenny ready to order?" George asked, as he came around the counter. He pulled his orderpad from the pocket of the white apron that encircled his ample girth. He and his customer walked back to Jenny and Chip, and Josh sat down at the table.

Josh ordered the chicken-fried steak with mashed potatoes. "Zach said not to leave Turk without trying the cafe's specialty."

George laughed. "Yeah, Zach's put away a lot of Hazel's good dinners."

"After that big breakfast, I don't think I'd do a full meal justice. What's the soup today, George?" Jenny inquired.

"Vegetable beef. Homemade, of course."

"Of course," she agreed, knowing Hazel made everything from scratch. "A bowl for me, please, and Chip's favorite toasted cheese sandwich with a half-order of fries. Oh, a little dish of applesauce for him, too."

When George took their order to the kitchen, Josh apologized for talking so long with George.

"I wanted to meet the man who'd helped you with Bart and thank him," he explained. "He sure thinks the world of you, Jen."

"I'm really fond of George and Hazel, too. They were good friends of my folks years ago."

The door opened, and Jenny looked over her shoulder, not wanting to believe it could be Bart a second time. She smiled in relief when she saw the Lauterbacks, Joe and Becky, with their new baby girl.

"Hello, Becky," she called, catching her friend's eye and beckoning her over to their table.

"Hi, Jen," the petite, green-eyed blonde dressed in jeans and a windbreaker greeted her high school friend warmly. "Hi, Chip. How are you doing?" She nodded at Josh who rose from his chair courteously.

When Joe had joined his wife after dropping the diaperbag at their table, Jenny introduced her friends to Josh.

Josh shook hands with Joe, a man in his twenties, just short of six feet, with black hair and eyes.

"Glad to meet you, Brady. Beck and I'd heard through the grapevine that you'd come to visit." He gave Josh a friendly smile and a look that said he hoped he understood about small towns.

Josh grinned as well. "Yeah, it seems everyone's heard about me and where I come from."

Jenny had risen, too, to get a closer look at the baby, the Lauterbacks' first.

In reply to Jenny's question, Becky said, "Her name's Sara Ann." She proudly held her little girl in the crook of her arm and loosened the light blanket around her. Sara Ann waved her little hands in the air and gurgled. She was an adorable baby with her mother's blonde hair. "She's growing like a weed. We've come into town to shop and decided to have lunch to celebrate her turning six weeks old tomorrow."

The two men exchanged a smile. Anyone could tell Becky and Joe were proud of their new little daughter. Josh hoped, as he looked at the young family, that he and Jenny would have a little girl one day.

Jenny looked lovingly at the baby and had similar thoughts. She sighed, and said to Becky, "I'm sorry I haven't been out to see her, Beck. Things have been sort of hectic around the ranch."

"I understand, Jen. So much has happened recently," she added. "You've become a mother yourself, now. Is it going to work out, do you think?" She gave Jenny's arm a gentle squeeze.

"Yes. Chris's will named me as guardian, and the county has finally approved me. I'm so relieved to have it settled!"

"Good for you. I wish you the best of luck," her friend said, and Joe agreed.

Becky stooped to give Chip a look at her daughter, and he gazed curiously at her for a moment, then squealed, "Look, Jen-jen, baby! Pretty!"

The adults laughed, and Joe commented, "I wonder if he'll think that about twenty years from now," which brought another round of laughter.

George arrived with the lunches, and the Lauterbacks excused themselves to go to their booth.

"Nice people. Have you known them long?" Josh asked after a few minutes of sampling Hazel's cooking.

Jenny poured some catsup for Chip's fries before replying.

"Yes, Becky graduated a year ahead of me. Joe is a few years older. They live northeast of town on a farm next to his father's place. Joe farms both properties, I think."

"They seem very happy," Josh observed.

"I hope they are. Becky's adored Joe since she was a kid, and somewhere along the way, he must have noticed her, too, because they got married when he finished college. She worked in the school office before the baby's birth."

"Well, Chip's right. That baby is sure a pretty little thing."

"Maybe Chip's going to have a thing for blondes," she chuckled from behind her hand, as if she didn't want Chip to hear.

"Could be," Josh drawled, "but I tend to like long, black hair, and blue eyes that sparkle, even when I'm not with the beautiful woman who owns them."

"I'm not used to being sweet-talked."

He looked at her across the table. *This girl is so lovely, and yet to think no one had ever sweet-talked her before. What's the matter with the men around here?*

"I meant it, Jenny."

That brought a wash of pink to her cheeks, and she busied herself with helping Chip manage his applesauce.

After Josh had decided she wouldn't reply, she said quietly, "Thank you for the compliment, Josh. It's nice to hear such sweet words and," in a rush of honesty, "I admire you, too." *Oh, no,* she thought, *where did those words come from? They sounded so stilted and so—so prim!*

Josh watched her fuss with the boy, not quite sure how to read her, then finished his coffee.

"If you've finished your soup, I'll pay the bill. I'd like to drive out to that lake you mentioned. Is it pretty out there?"

Glad to talk about something neutral, she agreed, "Very pretty. I'll take Chip to the restroom and join you shortly." She unstrapped the boy and held his hand as they walked to the back of the cafe.

Jenny helped Chip tiptoe to use the toilet. *With his long legs, he can almost do it by himself*, she thought. They joined Josh as he was coming out of the men's room.

"All set?" he asked and lifted the boy to his left hip.

"All set," she replied and swung her purse and the diaperbag over her left shoulder.

They briefly stopped by the Lauterbacks' booth to say goodbye, before walking to the car. Josh fastened Chip into the carseat, and they were on their way toward the lake.

"It *is* a pretty area," Josh commented as they neared the lake.

Jenny had pointed out, in passing, the Lauterbacks' home. She noticed in the rearview mirror that Chip had dropped off to sleep about halfway to the lake.

"Look," she whispered to Josh and motioned toward the backseat.

Josh smiled. "Out like a light."

"He's such a sweet little fellow," she commented.

"Yes, he is. Chris and Sue were doing a good job with him, and I have confidence that you will too." He paused, started to say something more, then stopped.

Jenny didn't notice it and just said, "Thanks." She followed a gravel drive that wound around the south and east sides of the lake. They passed several camping areas, a boat ramp, and a swimming beach.

"Good fishin'?" Josh asked.

"My dad thought so. He liked to get away up here, especially after Mom was gone. I fished with him sometimes, but I don't have a talent for it."

"There are a lot of lakes in my part of North Texas. Real pretty like this one. I'd like to show my place to you, Jen. Do you think you'd like to come down some time?" he asked as he glanced at her face. She was intent on following a circular loop, and re-traced the way they'd come.

After a moment or two, she answered, "Yes, I think I'd like that."

Josh let out the breath he'd been holding. He felt relieved that she'd agreed to that much. There was hope for a future with her.

They were nearing the parking lot for the swimming beach when Josh said, "Pull in here, Jen. Let's walk a bit. I figure Chip'll sleep for a while, don't you?"

She did as he'd asked. Rolling a window down a few inches for air for Chip, and so they'd hear him if he did wake up, she laid a light blanket over him as he slept in the carseat. She and Josh walked down a path that sloped toward the beach, then through the sand to the water's edge.

Jenny breathed deeply of the fresh air and, shading her eyes with one hand, looked across the lake toward steep cliffs that lined the opposite shore.

"See the cliffs over there? A drive leads out to them, and it's a favorite parking spot for local teenagers . . . I'm told," she added guilelessly.

Josh guffawed. "Now, Jen, you expect me to believe you've never been parking up there?"

"Well," she paused as she watched a fisherman putt-putt by in the middle of the lake. The lake had a limit of 5 horsepower motors, but the motorboat still set up a pleasant lap of water at their feet. "A couple of times," she admitted.

Josh had squatted down to trail the fingers of his right hand through the cold, lapping water. He glanced up at her with a glint in his caramel eyes. "No guy tried to be your boyfriend? Hard to believe, girl."

"Well, believe it, cowboy. I think they all liked and respected Chris too much to want to mess with his sister. I remember my father looking at me once when I was all dressed up for church and saying, 'One of these days, Jenny, I'm going to have to beat the boys off with a stick!' That never really happened, of course, but I guess that was his way of telling me he thought I was pretty."

Josh rose to stand beside her. "Sounds that way. I'll bet he was real proud of his beautiful daughter, and sorry that he had to leave you so early on."

She nodded and whispered, "I imagine so."

"Jenny," Josh murmured, as he put his right arm lightly around her waist. "You know, I think I'm in love with you."

A gasp escaped her parted lips, and she turned and looked up at him in astonishment and more than a little panic.

"But, you don't know me very well—you've been here such a short time," she said disbelievingly. "I—I—but what—how do you know? How does a person tell?"

She stopped, suddenly embarrassed by her own babbling. *Why do I do that? Sometimes the words just tumble all over each other.*

"I'm not sure I can answer that, Jen. I just know that the feelings I have for you are different from what I've felt for anyone else. I've done my share of dating, and a few times, I even thought that maybe I'd met the right one, but it never worked out. I've been very lonely, but I feel now that that was meant to be, because what I feel now for you is so much stronger, sweetheart, more real than anything I ever felt before.

"It's not just your beauty and grace; it's who you are inside. Your compassion, your spunkiness; I even like your stubbornness."

He looked into her eyes, and paused.

"Please, honey, say something. Am I explaining myself well enough? Or am I digging a hole I can't climb out of? Give me a hint."

She did. She raised her hands around his neck. "Oh, Josh," she whispered.

"Thank you, Jenny." He murmured and gathered her closer into his arms, burying his face in her thick hair. "I knew I wanted to marry you the first day I was here. I came up to the house for the blankets and saw you sitting with Chip on your lap, reading to him. It hit me then, took my breath away. I knew I'd been looking for you all my life. I want you for my wife. I want to have a family with you."

He raised his head and kissed her gently. Then, in a voice gruff with deep emotion, said, "I think I just proposed to you, Jenny Courter."

He looked into her blue eyes, and saw wonderment, tenderness—but concern and doubt, as well. His heart fell into his boots, but he gulped and went on bravely.

"It's okay, Jen. I spoke too soon. I guess it's because I'm leaving tomorrow, and I didn't want to leave you without you knowing I love you."

"It makes me so happy to hear you love me, Josh. I think you're a wonderful man, so kind and thoughtful, so generous, too. I'll admit that when you came around the corner of my house that day,

I thought you were about the handsomest cowboy
I'd ever laid eyes on. I think I fell for you right
then and there, without even knowing anything
about you. If it were just you and me, I'd say yes
this minute, but—but. . . ."

She stepped back a little and clasped her hands
before her at her waist.

"But too much has happened too quickly in my
life. I have so much to handle, and I'm concerned
I'd grow to rely on you. I need to stand on my
own two feet."

She paused and paced back and forth in the
sand, while she chose her words.

"Being a mother is so new to me—I want to
do a good job. I owe it to Chris and Sue. Would
getting married now be the best thing for Chip?
Would it be good to uproot him now and take him
to Texas to live—because how could you live up
here? There are so many things to consider. Do
you understand, Josh?"

Josh saw the turmoil in her eyes, and he sought
to alleve it. He loved her too much to see her
hurting.

"Of course, honey. Getting married is probably
the most important decision anyone makes in life,
and I'd want it to be for life, if we marry. I think
you may feel the same?"

She nodded mutely.

"I figured so. Look, Jen, you can take as much

time as you need to think it over. I've told myself many times these past few days to go slow. But, I couldn't keep quiet any longer. I wanted you to know what's in my heart."

She moved closer to hug him, and he enveloped her in a bear hug.

"My sweet Jenny."

When he released her, she looked at him soberly with still a hint of disbelief in her blue eyes.

"I'm honored that you want me for your wife. I just can't believe you'd choose me. I must admit that the idea of marrying kind of panicks me. I've always looked at it as something far down the road for me. But I'll try to give you an answer soon, Josh."

"I can't ask for more than that, Jen. You think about it, and when you're ready we'll talk over the questions you have," he replied.

They turned to walk hand-in-hand slowly back to the car. He knew they could work it out; she was just feeling a bit overwhelmed right now. *Please let her say yes,* Josh silently prayed.

When they returned to the ranch, Josh saw Jenny and Chip into the house. Wanting to leave her alone to think—he hoped about him—he excused himself to go to the barn to see if he could help Zach with anything.

"Since it's my last afternoon here," he said, and

felt renewed hope when a sad look crossed her face.

He found Zach cleaning up the tackroom. He greeted Josh warmly.

"Back so soon? Thought you might be gone all afternoon," he observed with a smile.

"Dang it, Zach. I think I blew it."

Josh plopped down on a bench and leaned forward, elbows on his thighs, while he worried his Stetson in his hands.

Chapter Twelve

Zach propped his broom in a corner and sat opposite Josh on an old wooden chair, prepared to listen.

"What's happened, boy?"

Josh gave a disgusted grunt, slapped his hat down onto the bench beside him, and answered gloomily, "I asked her to marry me."

"Well, now, I'm not surprised at that, knowing how you feel about her," the man replied, trying to hide a little smile.

"Yeah," Josh agreed morosely, "but I jumped the gun. She sort of panicked about making such a big decision so soon after everything that's happened."

Zach inserted, "I can believe that. Jen's been

trying hard to be independent, take charge and make the right decisions for Chip and the ranch."

"I knew that, which is why I should've kept my big mouth shut," Josh berated himself. "But, I didn't want to leave without her knowing I love her, and before I knew it, I was proposing."

"Did she say a flat-out no?" Zach asked gently.

"No, not exactly. She even said she might love me, too, but she's not sure how to tell if it's the real thing. That surprised me, Zach."

The older man sat quietly, rubbing his chin in thought, then said, "Jen's real pretty, and boys have come around but she's never paid them much mind. I'd bet she's never been in love, so maybe she doesn't trust her judgment on that score."

"Yeah, she said that to me when she tried to explain," Josh agreed, "but it's hard to wait, knowing I'll be gone tomorrow. What if she never wants me to come back again?"

He rose from the bench and restlessly walked to the window and looked toward the house. "I couldn't take that."

Zach walked up behind him and clasped his left shoulder in a firm grip. "Now don't get down on yourself. Just give her some time."

Josh nodded. "Thanks for listening, Zach." He picked up his hat and added, "If there's nothing pressing for me to help you with, I think I'll take Vanguard out for one last ride."

"Go on, then," the old man replied.

He stood looking out the window, deep in his own thoughts, until he heard Josh and the stallion leave the horse barn. A few minutes later, he ambled up to the house. He found a worried-looking Jenny sitting in the kitchen rocker while she watched Chip play near his toybox.

She looked up, startled by his sudden appearance, then blurted out, "Oh, Zach! Josh asked me to marry him, and I—I have to decide. He's not pressuring me, I don't mean that. I think I love him, but how do I know for sure? I just don't know if I'm ready for such a big step, and I can see so many problems down the road. Where do we live? Josh has a ranch *and* a business in Texas, but I love this place, and I want Chip to learn to love it, too. How can he do that if he grows up in Texas?"

She got up, and Zach gave her a hug.

"Well, Jen, if you're asking my advice, probably the best path to follow is your heart. If you love each other, you need to be together, and anything can be worked out as long as the love is there. You and he should be doin' some serious talkin'."

Maybe I should take my own advice, he thought.

" 'He's just an old man, what does he know?' you're probably thinkin'. But, you know I had a wife once, and I think that boy loves you as much as I loved my Mattie, and that was a heck of a lot, my girl. Now, why don't you saddle up Ricci and head out across the pastures to the east. If you try, you'll find Josh and Vanguard out there somewhere."

Jenny looked up into his wrinkled face and thought how lucky she was to have this man, her friend and surrogate parent.

Swiping the back of her hand over her teary eyes, she thanked him and ran to the backporch. Turning, she began to speak, but Zach read her thought.

"Go ahead, Jen. I'll stay with Chip."

She flashed him a huge smile, grabbed her hat and denim jacket and tore down the path to the horse barn.

In the meantime, Josh rode Vanguard off toward the east end of the ranch, thinking he'd go through the gate and explore the lower reaches of the Madison Range. Zach had shown him the gate once when the two men had ridden out together. He'd been riding the stallion hard, releasing some of his tension over Jenny, when he topped a rise and decided to rest the horse for a few minutes.

"I shouldn't push you, old boy," he murmured

to Vanguard as he leaned forward and patted his warm, damp neck. "Not your fault my nerves are on edge."

He stayed in the saddle and looked around him. Off to the south a stream meandered out of a small valley on its way to join Turk Creek. The creek formed part of the boundary line between the ranch and the neighboring High Meadows Ranch. *Hadn't noticed that little valley before,* he thought.

Vanguard suddenly whinnied and looked back the way they'd ridden. Josh turned and looked, too. A rider was coming toward them. It took only a moment for Josh to tell that it was Jenny on her palomino, riding at a steady pace. When she saw Josh astride Vanguard, silhouetted against the blue sky, she waved and prodded Ricci to a gallop.

Josh urged Vanguard down the hill toward her, and the strong horses quickly closed the space between them.

The riders reined in when they reached each other, and Josh asked, a note of apprehension in his voice, "What's wrong, Jen? Has something happened at the house?"

"Oh, no, Zach and Chip are okay," she answered as she held Ricci steady. The mare danced sideways. "I—I wanted to see you. I—we need to talk, don't we?" She stammered a bit in her excitement.

Josh reached over and took her hand. "Yeah, we do, honey. But for a minute there, I thought the barn was on fire, or something."

Jenny grinned. Josh had a way of saying just the right thing to ease her anxiety. "No fire," she explained, "I was just eager to find you. Zach came up to the house and told me you were taking Vanguard out for a last ride. I wanted to be with you."

The handsome stallion took advantage of the situation and cozied up to Jenny's beautiful mare by rubbing his nose on her neck.

Josh laughed. "I think Vanguard's got the right idea," and he rose in his stirrups, reached and lifted Jenny from her saddle over to his own.

"Josh!" she protested, but didn't exactly discourage him either. Josh slipped backwards and settled her across his saddle, then took Ricci's reins in his left hand. The gentle mare turned and stood beside Vanguard.

"Now, honey, why did you want to find me so bad?" he asked, a warm gleam in his eyes as he looked down at the girl he loved.

Jenny snuggled close, her left arm around Josh, and his right supporting her back. She took a deep breath, and said, "I needed to tell you that I love you. I *do* love you, Josh. I didn't want you to go back to Texas without knowing that I do."

Josh let out a whoop that had the horses giving

him a look over their shoulders, but they held steady. Josh ducked his head and met Jenny's sweet lips as she moved to put her arms around his neck. She quickly grabbed her hat as Josh, in his eagerness, had knocked it back.

"I love you, too, Jen. You've made me very happy. I was so worried I'd leave tomorrow, and you'd never want me to come back again." He emphasized his words with a hug. "But you're right, we need to talk about a lot of things. Where should we go? Back to the house?"

After a moment's thought Jenny said, "Turn Vanguard toward that stream over there." She indicated the same stream Josh had noticed earlier. "I want to show you my favorite place on the whole ranch. Ricci and I often ride up that little valley. Here, let me remount, and I'll lead the way."

Josh gave her one last hug and boosted her over to her mare's back. Jen settled her hat and urged Ricci forward.

A half mile up the valley, Jenny said over her right shoulder, "Here it is, Josh. My special place."

The two of them dismounted and left the horses to graze, while they walked out onto the rock outcropping that Jenny loved.

"This is a nice spot, Jen. It's a pretty little valley," he added admiringly.

"I found it years ago when I was first allowed to ride out on my own. I've always come here when things got to be too much, or I wanted to think. Ricci's been a patient listener to my troubles over the years."

"I'm glad you have her, Jen. There's a spot on a hill at the Brady Belle, that I've always liked to ride to. I sit under a big old pecan tree and think about things. I can look back and see the house and all the other buildings spread out below me. Makes a pretty picture. I look forward to riding up there with you, honey."

Jenny smiled in agreement and hugged him about the waist.

"The sun's nice and warm," he noted, as he took off his jacket.

She removed hers as well. They sat down, Josh with his back against a boulder, his knees drawn up. He settled Jenny between them, her back to him. She took off her hat, and he rested his head on her soft hair, when she leaned back against him. "This is nice," he whispered near her ear.

"Yes, it is," she returned.

"I believe spring has finally come to Montana, at least for today," she kidded, knowing how changeable the weather could be.

"What did Zach say that made you come riding after me, hon?" Josh asked.

"He's such a dear, wise man. He said if I loved

you and you loved me, the important thing is to be together. That together we can work anything out." She ducked her head and kissed his hand. "He also said that he thought you loved me as much as he'd loved his wife, Mattie, once, and that was one heck of a lot. So he urged me to do some serious talking with you."

"Bless Zach," Josh said. "And there is a lot to talk about. Where do we start?"

She shifted in his arms, so she could see his face.

"What worries me is how can you marry me and live and work in Texas?" she asked with a frown on her brow.

"Oh, there are ways to do that. Nowadays, it's quick to get back and forth. In fact, I flew up here on our corporate jet, and Tony and Jay, the company pilots, will pick me up tomorrow."

Jenny's eyes widened in astonishment, and she commented, "My goodness. I've never known someone who had their own jet."

Josh hugged her and laughed, "Oh, sweetheart, it's not mine. It belongs to Starr Enterprises, so it's available to me, but it's also used by other board members and key employees when needed."

Jenny smiled, a little pink-cheeked, and said, "You'll have to forgive my lack of knowledge about things like that. You're dealing with a smalltown girl here."

"Well, I don't look at you that way, Jenny. You're lovely and charming, bright and intelligent, and I'll be proud to have you on my arm when I have to attend those boring business dinners and such."

"I imagine we'll have to entertain sometimes, too?" Jenny asked, the apprehension in her voice not missed by Josh.

"Yes, some. But don't fret about it. We'll go slow with the social scene. I like quiet evenings at home best."

"Good. I want you mostly to myself anyway," she grinned. "I'll bet there'll be plenty of Dallas women who'll stare daggers into my back, when they learn you got married."

Josh smiled, "Now, I don't know about that, but you just remember that you're the one I love. Don't ever doubt it, sweetheart."

They sat quietly for a few minutes, both thinking of the future and all it could hold for them.

"I wanted to ask you," Josh began, "if I could have a dedicated phone line put in here at the ranch for a fax hook-up. That way, when I'm in Montana, Emily can fax me papers to read and sign, so I can stay on top of business down there. We've a fax machine at the Brady Belle, too, so Gabe can get in touch quickly if there's a problem I should know about."

"Of course. Anything you need to do, just do it. Especially if it keeps you here with me more."

"Good, and I want to be with you as much as possible, but I have to go back tomorrow as planned. I've put a deal on hold while I've been here, and I need to spend time on that. Then, there's a couple of construction sites I want to visit personally."

"I'll miss you while you're gone," she whispered.

"I'll miss you, too, hon, and Chip and Zach. I'd been hoping I could make it back by Chip's birthday. Which day is it?"

"End of the month. May 29th."

"Okay, I'll plan on that. You'll be ready to herd the cows to summer pasture about then, too, so I'll stay a while. Zach says Tillie wants to watch Chip so you can help drive the herd with Zach and me."

"My goodness, how nice of them to think of that. I'm so lucky to have them and you, Josh."

"Not half as lucky as I am to have found you, sweetheart," he told her.

She snuggled against him and sighed contentedly.

"Jenny, I told you I wanted to ask you to marry me almost from the first time I saw you. You may think I made up my mind too fast, but that's not the case. I've known for years the kind of girl I hoped to find—one that would love the land and living on a ranch as much as I do. But there's more to it."

He paused and touched a finger to her lips, when she started to speak.

"Just hear me out. Remember I told you that Chris showed me Sue's picture not long before he left the circuit? Well, he also showed me your picture. His wallet was open on the table, and I asked who the cute kid was." Jenny smiled. "He told me. It was the first I'd known of you. You were fourteen, with long, black braids hanging over your shoulders wearing a white hat. But it was your gorgeous blue eyes that grabbed me the most. They seemed to just tug at me, like they could pull me in. It's been seven years, but I've never forgotten how looking into your eyes made me feel. And that was just a picture, so imagine how looking at the real girl makes me feel."

Jenny exclaimed, "Seven years ago? That's amazing!" She lovingly stroked his left cheek. "You truly mean it?"

"Yes. I've never meant anything more. So, maybe that helps you understand why I hope we can be married really soon . . . like tomorrow?" he teased.

Jenny smiled again. "I'd marry you tomorrow, if only we could figure out how to manage to combine our lives. I'd move with you to Texas, but I need to keep the ranch going for Chip's sake. It's his inheritance. Besides it means a lot to me, too."

Josh hugged her close and stroked her hair back from her face. The afternoon breezes had picked up.

"I understand, Jen. We both love our land, and it's important to do what's best for Chip. So, I've been thinking that we should spend part of the year at each place. As you already know, I have a house in Dallas that was my grandfather's, and I'm there most of the time because of work, but I get out to the ranch as much as possible. Gabe runs the ranch with the help of hired hands. We can trust Zach to run this place for you, I'm sure."

She interrupted him to agree. "Yes, I'd trust him completely. He loves this land as much as I do. He's made his home here since before I was born."

"I think if we hired some trustworthy people to help here, he could handle things even though he's getting up in years," Josh suggested.

Jenny's face showed him how much she liked that idea.

He continued, "And we could spend part of our time up here, not just to help Zach, but so little Chip can grow to feel a part of the Courter family place as he gets older."

"Oh, Josh, that's a wonderful plan. Thank you

for considering my feelings about this place, and Chip, too. Are you sure you don't mind getting a bride with a ready-made family?"

Josh laughed and hugged her again.

"Jen, I love Chip already. When we visited Chris's grave, I made a pledge to him that I'd do all that I could to support the boy and you in anything you wanted to do. I meant it with all my heart. Besides, I wouldn't care if you had half a dozen little ones in tow. I'd gladly take them all home with me, just as long as you came, too."

Jenny whispered, "Josh, you're so sweet. I love you dearly, and I can't wait to be your wife." He turned her in his arms and kissed her.

"I'm here for you, sweetheart, now and forever."

Josh was proud that Jenny wasn't afraid to tell him that she wanted to be his wife. He knew in his heart that they would be happy together.

Josh took a deep breath and let it out. "You know, after waiting all these years for you, sweetheart, I want to do things right. Would you like to be married in that little white church you love?"

Jenny smiled happily. "Oh, yes, I *do* want us to be married there. I was baptized there and became a member while I was still a teenager. It's always been where I hoped to walk down the aisle as a bride, someday."

"Good. Then, that's the place for us. Any idea

when? Maybe a Saturday in June?" He read her frown. "Too soon, huh. Okay, July? August?" He looked at her with a hopeful grin.

She laughed delightedly. "Not anxious, are you? Well, how about late July or early August? We need a little time to make all the arrangements, especially since plans will have to be made at both ends—Texas, and Montana."

"That's true. It just seems so far away."

"It'll go fast," she looked into his handsome face and smiled, her love for him showing on her pretty face. "I want you to know that I love you very much, and I—I'll be the best wife to you that I can, and I'll try to make you happy."

"Oh, sweetheart," Josh murmured, as he pulled her close again. "We'll be very happy together. You're such a kind, decent woman. I'm a very lucky man! And, I'll be the best husband to you that I can, too."

He chuckled softly, and Jenny pulled back and looked at him.

"What are you thinking?" she asked, smiling in return.

"We'll have to ride up here often. It's a very special place, you know. We should remember it as the place we agreed to love and care for one another, right here under the beautiful Montana sky."

"I think that's a wonderful idea," Jenny said.

Yes, this place, that had always been so special to her, would have even more meaning. After all the bad things that had happened, she had been blessed with this wonderful, loving man. She leaned forward, took his face between her hands, and kissed his lips tenderly. Her own Texas cowboy.

They talked for a few more minutes, then rode back to the barn. Zach was very pleased to hear that they had decided to marry, and wished them all the happiness in the world.

Chapter Thirteen

Jenny and Josh found it difficult to say good-bye the next morning. He loaded his luggage into the Jeep, while Jenny, Chip and Zach waited nearby. Josh shook Zach's hand, then hugged him warmly.

Zach said gruffly, "Now, take care, boy. I'll be lookin' forward to when you can get back."

"Me, too. I'll see you at the end of the month. And, Zach, . . . thanks."

"You bet, son." He grinned and ambled off toward the barns, tactfully making himself scarce.

Josh took Jenny in his arms and kissed her as if he'd never let her go. She looped her arms about his neck.

"I'm going to miss you, sweetheart."

Tears in her eyes, Jenny agreed with a nod of her head. She rose on tiptoe and kissed him lovingly in return.

They stood for awhile, just holding one another, until Josh felt little Chip hugging his knee. He loosened his hold on Jenny, reached for the boy, and lifted him up. Jenny and Josh hugged Chip between them, and Josh kissed the boy's cheek.

"Bye, Chip. I have to take a trip now, but I'll be back soon. We'll have fun then, won't we?"

"Yep, fun!"

Jenny added, "Josh will come back for your birthday, Chipper, and we'll have a birthday party."

"Come back, Jo-ssh," the boy said and grinned at the man.

"I will, big fellow." Josh set Chip down and hugged Jenny again. "I've got to be on my way, honey. I'll call you this evening."

"I'll be here, cowboy," she replied, giving him a wide smile. Her blue eyes still glistened with tears, and she wiped her fingers across them.

"No tears, sweetheart. I'll be back before we know it, and we both have a lot to keep us busy until then."

"I know, it's just hard to say good-bye."

"Don't I know it! I love you, darlin', now don't forget that."

"I won't, Josh. I love you, too." She knew she had never meant anything more.

After one last hug, Josh got into the Jeep and started the motor. Jenny picked up Chip and settled him on her left hip.

"Wave bye-bye, Chip," she urged, and the boy did.

The two of them watched and waved as Josh drove down the lane. As he turned left onto the road, he honked his horn, looked back toward the house, and wiped a few tears from his own eyes. He was on his way to Texas, but he left his heart with Jenny.

Despite Jenny's misgivings, the month flew by. She looked forward to Josh's evening phone calls. They exchanged the news of their days, made summer wedding plans, and got to know each other better through those daily conversations.

Down in Texas, Josh thoroughly enjoyed Emily's joyful reaction to his news. She'd been urging him to find the right girl and settle down for several years. She was delighted it had finally happened.

His first free weekend, Josh drove home to the Brady Belle to give Gabe and Consuela the happy news. They were overjoyed as well, and Consuela was especially pleased that they'd be having a little child in the house again.

Josh also caught up with his work at Starr Enterprises. The Broadwater deal went forward to his satisfaction, and a contract was drawn up to build an affordable housing complex in an area of the city that was undergoing major renovations. He and Mr. Broadwater agreed that affordable housing would *not* mean cheap construction. Ground was broken and the job underway, before Josh returned to Montana.

Back on the Courter Ranch, things moved along as well. The painting crew came out to paint the barns and, two weeks later, did a beautiful job on the house. Jenny was thrilled with how yellow paint with dark green trim breathed new life into the old ranch house . . . she just wished Sue could have seen it.

Arrangements were made to install a second phone line in the house. A few days after the line was installed, a delivery truck arrived with a state-of-the-art fax machine and copier. When Josh assured Jenny that if she faxed him, it would go to the machine in Emily's office only, she sent a daily note to him that he'd read first thing each morning when he arrived. It made his day. And, also, made him even more anxious to get back to her. He faxed notes in return, which Jenny took up to her bedroom to be read and re-read before she fell asleep each night.

* * *

The first Saturday in August, at exactly three o'clock in the afternoon, Jenny stood in the vestibule of the church, her arm linked through Zach's. Chip, Tillie and Beth waited with them. Speaking in hushed tones, they encouraged one another not to be nervous.

Zach cleared his throat and ran a finger under his stiff white collar. His black bolo tie moved a bit as he swallowed.

"I'm proud to walk you down the aisle, Jen, even if I am nervous. You sure do look beautiful."

Jenny laughed and hugged his arm. "Thank you, Zach. I'm nervous, too, but I'm so happy . . . I just can't find the words."

She did, indeed, look beautiful. Tillie, Beth, Chip and she had spent a wonderful Saturday in late June shopping for the perfect dress. Jenny had a mental image of the type she wanted, and she found it.

Made of white silk organza, the fitted bodice was an off-the-shoulder style, accented with a silk rose at the dip of the neckline. The full skirt was bustled with a cluster of more white silk roses. Tiers of lace cascaded from under the bustle to encircle the hemline. The toes of her new white boots could be glimpsed as she moved.

A white Western-style hat, adorned with a large, white silk rose on the brim, held a softly pleated tulle hatband that flared into a short veil.

Under the veil, her hair tumbled free in waves, just as Josh liked it. She wore the opal and diamond pendant that he had given her, and she carried a bouquet of yellow roses. Josh was touched by her selection of yellow roses for the men's boutonnieres, and the women's bouquets. Jenny thought it the perfect way to honor her Texas cowboy's home state.

In reality, the bridal couple had no family but for Jenny's little nephew. But the church was filled with neighbors and friends. Tony Hidalgo had flown the jet up from Dallas on Friday afternoon, bringing with him Josh's secretary, Emily, and her husband, as well as Gabe and Consuela Martinez. Josh honored that couple by seating them as his surrogate parents, and Jenny honored Zach and Tillie in the same way. Joe Lauterback had just ushered Consuela and Gabe to their seats in a front pew and returned for Tillie.

Tillie looked elegant in a green silk sheath under a matching short-sleeved jacket adorned by her corsage of yellow roses. She patted Jenny's arm, whispered, "Good luck," and took Chip's hand as Joe escorted them down the aisle. Chip called, "Bye-bye," over his shoulder to the delight of the wedding guests.

In a few minutes, Beth followed them. She looked lovely in a calf-length chiffon dress in swirling tones of gold and copper. The colors wonderfully complimented her gorgeous red hair and golden eyes.

Jenny's first thought was to have her childhood friend and college roommate be in her wedding party, but Connie was spending an adventurous summer as an exchange student in Italy. So, instead, Jenny asked Beth to be her attendant. Beth thought herself too old at thirty-three to be in a wedding, but her fondness for Jenny and Chip overcame her reluctance.

Now, she slowly walked down the aisle with a fluttery stomach, smiling gently at Josh and his best man, as she approached the altar. Josh heard a low murmur, something in Spanish, from Tony who stood at his left. He noticed Beth turned pink-cheeked suddenly. Then, the organist signaled the approach of the bride, and Josh's complete attention was riveted on the end of the aisle.

Jenny took a deep, steadying breath, exchanged a happy smile with Zach, and stepped through the double doors into the sanctuary. Though she returned the smiles of their guests, her eyes focused on her handsome Texas cowboy, looking gorgeous in a black tux, black bowtie and pleated white shirt.

Josh's breath caught at the sight of his beautiful Jenny in her wedding gown, but he met her smile with one of his grins. Suddenly, he was no longer nervous, just exceedingly grateful that Jenny was about to become his bride. Seeing that grin put Jenny at ease, too, and the horde of butterflies dancing in her stomach settled down.

Zach placed her hand in Josh's and took his seat next to Tillie. Chip promptly climbed onto his lap.

Jenny and Josh turned to the pastor and the ceremony that would join them in a marriage that would last for the remainder of their lives.

Josh and Jenny took a Caribbean cruise for their honeymoon. They then stayed a few days in Dallas where he enjoyed showing her around the city. They also fixed up a bedroom for Chip in Josh's house. It was a three-story Victorian set on a large lot across from the Starr Building. Jenny fell in love with the house on sight and agreed with Josh that it was the perfect place to raise a family.

Two weeks after their wedding, the newlyweds were back in Montana.

Tillie had stayed in Jenny's old bedroom at the ranch and cared for Chip, taking him to Beth's daycare while she did her post office duties.

Tillie invited Zach, Chip and the Bradys to her home one fine August evening, not long after their return. To Josh and Jenny's surprise, it was a celebratory dinner, not just for them, but for Zach and Tillie, as well.

As they enjoyed the excellent food, and Tillie

had served coffee and peach pie for dessert, Zach cleared his throat, and began to speak.

"While you kids were gone, Tillie and I took advantage of the extra time we were spending together, her stayin' at the ranch and all, and we've gotten to know each other better.

"Now, I know we're gettin' up in years, and probably some of the folks around here will think we're crazy, but I've asked Tillie to marry me." He paused and took Tillie's left hand in his right, as she sat next to him at the dining table.

That sweet lady smiled happily across the table at Jenny and Josh as she squeezed Zach's hand in return.

"And I said yes."

Josh and Jenny looked at each other, astonished at the news, but delighted, too.

"Oh, my!" Jenny exclaimed, "I'm just thrilled, Tillie, and Zach, you've certainly kept this news quiet the couple of days we've been home."

She jumped up and rounded the table, as did Josh. A round of hugs were exchanged, and Josh pumped Zach's hand.

"This is wonderful news, and I hope Jen and I had a little bit to do with you two getting together."

"You had a lot to do with it, boy," Zach replied with a smile. "I'd still be just *thinkin'* about askin'

Tillie out to supper, if you hadn't encouraged me not to waste any more time."

Tillie and Jenny laughed.

"I guess I have you to thank then, Josh," Tillie said and planted a big kiss on his cheek.

"Hmmm," Jenny kidded, "I didn't know you had such matchmaking skills, Josh."

"Hey, I matched us up, didn't I, sweetheart?" he exclaimed with a hug for his bride.

Amidst the laughter, Chip, who had been concentrating on his half piece of peach pie, suddenly yelled, "Done."

He went to the truck Jenny had brought along with them, and the adults sat down to finish their desserts and coffee.

"Now, tell us all your plans," Jenny suggested. "Have you set a date for the wedding?"

"Well, not exactly, but soon," Zach said with a grin.

Tillie laughed and swatted him on the arm. "I've put in for my retirement from the postal service. It'll happen the end of November, so if you kids can be back up here for a spell at Christmas, we'll plan the wedding then."

"Yep, we want you two to stand up with us," Zach said.

"Oh, I'd like that very much," Jenny agreed.

"Me, too. I'd be honored to be your best man, Zach."

Jenny looked at Josh. "We'd planned to spend Christmas in Montana already, hadn't we? This'll make it even more special."

"Where are you planning to live after you're married?" Josh asked, wondering if this would affect Zach's running the ranch.

Tillie answered, "Whoever is appointed the new postmaster will have the option of setting up the post office in another location. But, perhaps he'll want to keep it here. If I can't sell the house, there's always the choice of keeping it as a rental."

"Either way, Tillie's movin' out to the ranch with me," Zach inserted. "We think we can manage in the bunkhouse."

The newlyweds looked at each other. Jenny gave Josh a nod of her head, leaned over and whispered in his ear.

He grinned. "I agree, hon. We have a proposition for you two. We'd like you to live in the house. You can make the downstairs bedroom yours, and use any other parts of the house you'd like."

"But, that's your house, Jen," Tillie protested.

"It's a big house, Tillie dear, and when Josh, Chip and I come to spend time here, we'll help fill it up. But, while we're in Texas, it'd make me very happy to know the old house isn't sitting empty."

"That's very generous, kids," Zach said.

"Not at all," Josh added. "And this will free up the bunkhouse for the hired hands you'll need with both Jen and me away."

"That's true," Tillie agreed.

Zach looked at her and smiled. "You don't think we'll get lost rattlin' around in that big house?"

"I'll keep track of you, old man," Tillie returned with a laugh that made her hazel eyes sparkle.

Jenny thought her friend had never looked prettier, and she was so happy to know that Zach and Tillie had decided to marry.

On their last afternoon before they were to return to Dallas, Jenny put Chip down for his nap. Josh had asked Jenny to join him at the horse barn when he took his nap. When she got there, Zach excused himself to go up to the house, saying he'd look out for Chip for awhile.

Jenny looked questioningly at Josh. "What's going on, cowboy?" Zach looked like he was up to something. "Or are *you* the one who's up to something?" she added with a smile.

Josh had both Vanguard and Ricci saddled and ready for an afternoon ride.

He just smiled and asked, "Would you like to ride to your very favorite place on the whole ranch?"

Her blue eyes dancing, she replied, "Yes. One last visit to our little valley would be very special, before we head for Texas."

"Let's ride, sweetheart."